To Louise

Chained
DI Amelia
Barton of the
NCA
Book 3

my union sister.

Nicky Downes

Nicky Downes

Chained
©2021, **Nicky Downes**
Self-published
Nicjaydownes@gmail.com

Other works by the same author
Bat Girl
Traffic
Consent

Dedicated to all of the key workers who worked tirelessly to ensure that we were all safe during the most difficult of times.

Chapter 1

Discovery

"The first cases in the UK of this extraordinary virus have been confirmed today in York."

Johnny's Alsatian hadn't stopped barking between each radio news broadcast. At least there were no neighbours to hear the commotion. But Johnny's nerves jangled. He would show his stupid dog that unacceptable behaviour didn't go unpunished.

He zipped up his green bomber jacket before leaving the hut, then grabbed his torch. It might have been the tail-end of winter, showing the first sprigs of spring, but at 3:00 in the morning there was a distinctly icy chill in the air.

Simba lay down as he approached, ears flattened against his skull, knowing he was likely to get a rollicking. Johnny didn't come out of the hut without good reason.

"This better be good, boy."

Johnny grabbed the long, silver chain attached to his dog's collar and pulled the dog to his feet.

"Well?" Johnny demanded, getting into the dog's face. Simba's rotten breath caused him to turn away.

He hadn't noticed it at first but, just where the dog's legs had been previously been, lay half an arm… a woman's slender arm with a delicate wrist. Johnny stepped back, dropping the chain. He ran to the hut, grabbed his phone and dialled 999.

"I've found an arm in my yard. Yes, just an arm — a human arm."

Chapter 2

A Body

Amelia sat at her favourite desk facing the window. She'd received another email that morning informing her that she should use any available desk in the office at West Midlands Regional Organised Crime Unit. None of them was assigned for her sole use. *Balls to that!* She shot the message into the deleted folder.

This desk had a view of the fields. It was her desk and not one of her co-workers dared question that. She might as well take the opportunity to relax in her usual space, something that she'd found impossible to do over the past six months. At work, new cases came in. More women were discovered in the backs of airless lorries. These included more from Southern and Eastern Asia than had been the pattern in the previous few years. Their families saved up thousands for them to be trafficked to the UK, to a job in a nail bar if they were lucky, or a brothel, or worse. DCI Pat Mackenzie may have to compile the NCA monthly reports, but Amelia had to read them, putting faces to names as she desperately tried to find links to known traffickers.

It didn't get any easier following the trail of lies.

At home, Callum had progressed from walking to running at top speed — another milestone that she'd missed. A few months ago, Jola, her nanny, had sent her a video of her son's first steps, which should have made her shriek with delight. Instead, it filled her with guilt. She hadn't seen either of her daughters' first steps either, her late husband, Joe, having that honour. It didn't get any easier being a mum and a detective inspector.

The screen on her phone lit up. A mobile number that she didn't recognise flashed up. She answered on the third ring.

"DI Amelia Barton." Blunt and to the point.

"We've got a body similar to the ones you had last year."

Amelia picked up a pen and notebook, gesturing to DS Catherine Brown as she did. "Go on."

"It's a young woman, probably Eastern European, with a rose tattoo on her shoulder. She's been found in an abandoned factory next to the cut."

"Cut?"

"Sorry, Birmingham and Fazeley Canal. Just off Spaghetti Junction."

"We'll be there soon as. Address?"

The derelict building, large and unappealing, appeared to have lain empty for many years but still managed to retain an industrial elegance. The windows were tall and curved, mainly filled with shattered glass in jagged patterns. Amelia wondered about the building's history. What had been stored in the vast empty space and how was it related to the canal it ran alongside?

The body of a young woman was propped on a chair, half an arm dangling, the blood congealed. The small quantity of blood on the concrete floor suggested that the amputation had taken place long after death. But Amelia wasn't a forensic pathologist, unlike the woman in the blue paper suit taking samples from the body.

"You must be DI Barton and...?" A young male detective stepped up and held out his hand for Amelia to shake. Amelia ignored him. He turned to Catherine.

Catherine didn't ignore him and, judging from his wince, returned his handshake with some force. "DS Brown."

"A security guard from across the road alerted us to the body. This isn't his patch, but his dog found the rest of the arm. Probably dragged over there by a rat."

"Nice," Amelia muttered. She couldn't take her eyes off the tattoo. It was the same as the others — a brand from their trafficker. "How long has she been here?"

The forensic pathologist stopped what she was doing and looked directly at Amelia. "Need to test these samples first but I'd say at least a few months."

It could be the work of Robert Davies, alias The Devil, then. He'd only been dead six months. It probably wasn't DI Branfield's work. He'd been banged up for longer than that. Branfield had been The Devil's accomplice and a fellow abuser of women.

"I need your best estimate, when you have it."

The young detective stepped forward. "Wait a minute. This is my patch, so any sharing —"

Amelia shot him a look, the same look she would give Becky, her eldest daughter, when she stepped out of line.

The detective stepped back. "But of course, I'll cooperate with you as best I can. If... if you think it's one of yours."

It was, without question. This poor woman had to be one of the women trafficked by The

4

Devil and his gang. They'd operated across Europe but were based in the Midlands. They owned brothels and clubs and exploited the vulnerable, both sexually and through drug running. Robert Davies was dead now, though. Michal, Amelia's lover, formerly a professional boxer, had killed him in her home — another cause of stress for her over the last six months.

But she'd almost forgotten these women, the murdered ones, each branded with the same rose tattoo. Amelia hated herself for thinking it would all come to an end when The Devil was killed. Maybe it had. Hopefully, this was the last, a hangover from his corrupt and evil empire. Amelia didn't believe so, though. The burning in her gut told her otherwise.

Catherine didn't speak as Amelia drove them back to WMROCU. Instead, she sat slumped in the passenger seat, constantly checking her phone.

Amelia felt annoyance creeping up her body. "Problem?"

Catherine sat up. "No. Nothing important." She quickly dropped her phone in her bag and patted the side of her braids.

"Kids okay?" Catherine had a few. Amelia couldn't remember how many. It could be more or less than her three, but they didn't talk about their families at work.

"Yeah, fine." Catherine furrowed her weaved eyebrows. "It's not them... doesn't matter. It'll resolve itself."

Amelia took one hand off the steering wheel and waved it in Catherine's direction. "If you ever need any help…" *Don't ask me. I've got enough problems of my own.*

Catherine just smiled then got her phone back out of her bag.

A few minutes later, Catherine muttered, "How many is it now?"

Amelia knew what she meant: how many dead, tattooed women? Two found at abandoned sites in Birmingham, including a derelict pub; one found on a swing at a park near Chelmsley Wood. Then there was Jola, her nanny, who had been trafficked into the country by The Devil, then literally torn apart and left for dead by DI Branfield as part of a sex game. He now languished in prison awaiting trial, a prospect that Amelia didn't look forward to and Jola dreaded.

Amelia's boss, DCI Pat Mackenzie, collared her as soon as she stepped out of the lift. "Another body?" she asked when they were behind closed doors. Pat had her own office. Amelia didn't even get her own desk. Amelia enjoyed the fieldwork, otherwise she'd put in for a promotion, but she hated being cooped up in an office. Compiling statistical reports would do her head in.

"Yeah, and branded just the same." Amelia waited for Pat to ask the next obvious question.

"Do you think he did it?" Pat chewed the end of her pen. "What's the timescale?"

"We're waiting on the pathologist for that. She reckoned the body was there for at least a few months."

"And no one had found it. Could have happened before his death, then. Can't count on it, though." Pat went back to her laptop. "Make sure you liaise with the lead DI."

This was another reminder that this was not Amelia's case to investigate. Her role ended at the trafficking. Murders were for the local murder squad. The detective in charge, who was young enough to be her son — *when did they get so young?* — may or may not keep her in the loop. Perhaps she should introduce him to her best friend, Carol, though she'd eat him for breakfast. The pair of them hadn't even managed a drink in recent times, the Public Protection Unit, where Carol worked as a DCI, being as busy as the NCA.

Catherine took the desk next to Amelia's. "Shall I open a new case file?"

Amelia opened her laptop. The Devil's case file was encrypted but sat on its own in her shared drive. It was labelled with his real name, Robert Davies, and was a different colour to all her other files in a bright red.

"No. Write it up in Davies' file. It all still links to him."

"Sure." But Catherine looked anything but sure.

"You think I'm wrong?"

"No..."

"Perhaps you think he hasn't killed anyone."

Catherine stared at Amelia and muttered, "I don't think that."

"Perhaps you think I'm obsessed with the bastard?"

Catherine grinned. "Well, now you come to mention it —"

"Yeah. You could be right. But add it as a subdirectory anyway. If he didn't do it, then someone he knows did."

It was late when they finished the paperwork. Amelia knew that her daily log would be scrutinised as the weekly briefing was the next morning and Pat loved to pick on her first. Women in the force had to show they were more competent than the men, especially if they had kids. It was an unwinnable game, but she kept dealing, hoping that one day she'd have the best cards to play. If she didn't have a good hand, the NCA wouldn't have touched her with a barge pole. Years of experience with the old-style Vice Squad had given her an edge over some other degree-touting recruits.

Catherine still appeared distracted and Amelia considered asking her for a drink or a meal before they went home to their respective broods. In the end, she decided she'd rather have a few moments saying goodnight to Callum and Caitlyn than eating with her silent, morose colleague.

Callum howled when she tried to pick him up off the floor. He had all his trains out and seemed to prefer smashing them into each other than giving his mum any attention. Amelia sighed and put him back down.

Jola looked up from the book she was reading. "His nappy needs changing before bed if you fancy it."

Amelia didn't, but at least that meant some closeness to her son before putting him down. Ignoring his protests, Amelia picked Callum up again and headed for the changing mat in the corner of the room. "Where's Caitlyn?"

"It's Monday. She's at boxing." Jola seemed engrossed and didn't raise her head.

Boxing. With Michal. Would he bring her home or get one of his sons to do it, as he had for the last two weeks? He couldn't make it more obvious that he didn't want to see her. But Caitlyn would be home in the next twenty minutes, so she'd find out then.

Callum seemed to enjoy the book she read to him perched on his cabin bed. He kept shouting, "Again, again!" He never bored of her reading the same pages over and over.

Amelia heard a car door slam. She kissed Callum on the top of the head. "Sleepy time now."

Then she lifted the corner of the blind so she could see into the street below. It was Michal's car. Amelia didn't waste any time in case he was just hoping to drop off her daughter and make a run for it. She got to the front door a few moments after he rang the bell.

Michal looked surprised to see her. "Amelia. How are you? I'm sorry —"

"Sorry?" Amelia stepped aside to let her daughter pass into the hallway. "You've got nothing to be sorry for. Why don't you come in for a drink?"

Michal shuffled his feet. Amelia expected him to make some excuse for having to leave and get home.

He surprised her. "It'll have to be coffee as I'm driving."

Amelia opened the door wider as Michal entered, nearly tripping over Caitlyn's gym bag. She'd dumped it in the middle of the hallway rather than bother to hang it up on the coat rack.

Whether it was the tension of having Michal nearby or just relief, Amelia had to stifle a giggle that formed deep in her chest.

Michal turned around. "You — you're laughing at me." He grinned.

It was that smile that had Amelia hooked at the start of their relationship. She didn't want to lose him. But what do you say to someone who killed a man to save you and your family? She owed him everything, but guilt consumed him. This smile had been a long time coming. Amelia hadn't seen him this relaxed in months.

Caitlyn was chattering animatedly to her nan and Jola, describing every punch and dodge of her evening. Rather than sit in the living room listening to the tale, Amelia led Michal into the kitchen. He sat at the breakfast bar and played with an errant spoon that her eldest daughter must have missed when loading the dishwasher. While Amelia made a fresh pot of coffee, he began to tap the rhythm of a recognisable song that Amelia couldn't quite place.

She walked over to Michal and placed her hand on his. He dropped the spoon. "I don't know why I'm nervous."

"A lot's happened."

Michal reached up and tucked a lock of her auburn hair behind her ear. Leaning his forehead on hers, he whispered, "God, I've missed you."

Caitlyn bounded in just at the wrong moment. "Can I have some orange juice?"

Amelia scowled but then softened. It wasn't her daughter's fault that she'd ruined the moment. Flicking the switch of the kettle, Amelia muttered, "Sure."

"Nan and Jola want a cup of tea." Caitlyn flew from the kitchen, her blonde ponytail bouncing behind her.

"She's doing well. She's got quite a right hook."

So we're back to the safety of boxing small talk.

"Great. I'm glad you're teaching her. But she still has so much energy left! Maybe you should work her harder."

Michal raised his eyebrows at this. "She'll always have plenty of energy. She has your genes."

Was he flirting? Amelia could never read the signs. If she'd had the courage, she'd have made a move on him right then but, instead, she leaned on the kitchen counter, a safe distance away, slurped her coffee and regaled him with tales of Callum's new adventures as a sprinter and climber. It wasn't long before he was glancing at his watch. She'd failed.

"Listen. I'd better get off. Why don't we go out for dinner soon? Ring me with some dates."

As if Amelia could ever plan anything. And he knew it.

Chapter 3
Briefing

Amelia hated the weekly briefing. The stuffy meeting room at WMROCU filled to the brim with testosterone. DCI Pat MacKenzie knew how to bring out the worst in her male counterparts. It had become a competition to see who could come out with the most outrageous claim, leaving Amelia cold and the other female officers fuming. It should have been nipped in the blood weeks ago and not allowed to get so out of hand.

When Amelia walked in, the first thing she noted was Pat standing at the front with her arms folded. A new case file was displayed on the interactive whiteboard with the ominous title: Operation Narrowboat. Whoever thought that one up must have been on drugs!

Amelia nodded at the screen. "I thought all operations had random names?"

Pat glanced over her shoulder then turned back to the room, scowling. "Okay. Which one of you changed it?'

Most of the men in the room covered their mouths and stifled a giggle – all except for Jason Starling, a civilian who had worked for the NCA even longer than Amelia. She had never heard him speak, let alone get involved in the office banter. He looked up, seemingly aware that Amelia was looking his way, and blushed.

Pat tapped the keys of the laptop, removing "Narrowboat" and changing it to "Caludon". Operation Caludon. It had a nice ring to it but it reminded Amelia of a Coventry landmark, Caludon Castle, so it surprised her that it had been chosen as an operational name. They were supposed to be unrelated to either force or type of case. She didn't mention it. It wasn't important but just reminded her that it was another part of Coventry, her hometown, that she'd never even visited. She must be the only mother in the city who had never even taken her kids to the Transport Museum.

The room was silent, waiting for Pat to speak. She wiped her hands on her trousers before beginning.

"Operation Caludon," she announced. The screen showed a photo of a warehouse like the one where the murdered woman had been found. "We've had intel from West Midlands Police that there's a human trafficking gang operating from this warehouse next to the Birmingham and Fazeley Canal."

"Is this the one where a woman's body was discovered yesterday?" Amelia interrupted.

"Not exactly. She was found half a mile away. But yes, on the same stretch of canal."

The next slide showed the second factory and a map indicating the distance between the two.

Amelia asked, "When are we raiding this warehouse?"

Pat looked straight at her and lowered her eyes. "We're not. At least not straight away."

Catherine interjected. "Why not? If we know there are trafficked people in there —"

"We need to find those at the very top of this gang or they'll just relocate." Pat still avoided looking either Amelia or Catherine in the eye.

"So, rather than free this group of potential slaves, we're going to watch them just in case we can catch a higher level of gangmaster?" Amelia knew how this worked but needed her boss to say it.

"Yes. We're going to start our surveillance tomorrow." Pat changed the slide to a picture of a rusting narrowboat.

The whole room erupted in laughter. Will muttered, "I know there've been cuts but surely this isn't the latest police transport…"

Pat blushed. "It makes sense. It has a great view of the place and we know that there are people arriving and leaving at all times of the day. A car or van would be noticed. There are no other occupied buildings close by that would afford a good view."

"So, you want us to carry out surveillance from a boat?" Catherine adjusted her expensive tailored jacket.

Amelia couldn't imagine her partner surviving a night in a three-star hotel, let alone on a cramped narrowboat next to a muddy towpath.

Pat passed out the rotas. She and Catherine were on the evening and night shifts. Two men from the Human Trafficking Division were on the daytime. Others would act as backup if needed. Catherine put down the sheet and immediately folded her arms. "Why are Amelia and I on nights? We've both got young families. Can't we swap?"

Pat sighed. "It doesn't fit the scenario. Your cover is that you're both cleaners, out during the day. Sean and Amir are going to be your boyfriends and working in security, so away during the night. If we stick to that then it won't raise suspicion."

Will butted in. "My parents have a narrowboat. You can't moor in the same place for more than two weeks unless you have a permanent mooring there."

"I know." Pat had clearly been briefed. "We've talked to the Canal and River Trust. They won't bother us. If we have any problems from other boaters, then you're to be rude enough to them to get them to leave you alone."

"And I thought the canals were supposed to be friendly." Amelia had heard that somewhere. The canals were supposed to be the friendliest part of the city and Birmingham had more of them than even Venice, apparently. She had no idea if either of these statements were true.

"This is the centre of Birmingham, not out in the sticks," Will pointed out, "so don't expect everyone to be on their best behaviour. You're also likely to meet some who, like your cover stories, have moved on to the canal because it's cheap accommodation."

"Oh, and before you all leave – we're expecting a shipment of hand sanitiser this afternoon, so make sure you help yourself to a bottle and use it regularly." Pat wrapped up the briefing.

But Will had to have the last word. "You'll need more than that if you're travelling through Birmingham locks."

Catherine and Amelia were pencilled in for narrowboat helmsmanship training in the morning. As they left the meeting room, Catherine shook the rota at Amelia. "What the fuck is helmsmanship? I was supposed to be going for a pizza with the kids tonight. Instead it'll be a trip to Go Outdoors to get wellies and suitable clothes."

Amelia couldn't help but grin at her partner. The thought of her handling dirty ropes while dressed in wellies and muddy jeans tickled her.

The full casework file was available on the shared drive when Amelia fired up her laptop. All of the previous hilarity was swept away in one swoop. The reports were grim reading.

One couple had reported to the police that they had come across a young woman of "oriental appearance" washing clothes in the canal. When she saw their narrowboat approaching, she had grabbed the basket of clothes and run away up a metal fire escape into the abandoned factory.

Amelia checked the date and time for the report – only three days ago at five in the morning. She read further into the report and saw that the couple were renting a narrowboat that had to be returned that evening and were behind schedule. Amelia doubted that you'd normally see anyone travelling along the canal at that time in the morning, so anyone wanting to keep themselves invisible could risk being outside.

The next report, dated last Monday, came from a homeless man. He'd spoken to the local PCSOs about seeing men entering the warehouse late at night. They left a few hours later. He further reported that he'd heard a woman crying. Were they using the warehouse as a brothel? Or were these men the traffickers?

The community officers weren't allowed to investigate the premises on their own so had reported it to the local police station. A report had been sent through to WMROCU and an order sent out to stay clear. Amelia squirmed in her seat. More than a week had gone by and nothing had been done to protect these women.

She didn't need to look at any other reports. Instead, Amelia stood, scraping her chair on the uncarpeted floor. She strode into

Pat's office. Without any pleasantries, she demanded, "Why the fuck aren't we getting these women out?"

"Take a seat, Amelia." Pat remained calm.

"Well?" Amelia sat on the chair nearest to Pat's desk.

"Coffee?" Pat was trying to disarm her.

"No, thanks."

Pat stood and walked over to the coffee machine and put in a pod. "Well, I'm having one."

"Okay then. Strong, black espresso, no sugar." Amelia crossed her legs, keeping the anger within her.

As soon as Pat sat down, arms out in front of her, she said, "I'm sorry you feel like this. And I understand your frustration, but we can't get those women, or possibly men, out yet."

"Men?"

"Yes, Amelia. We believe men are being kept there, too." Pat paused and raised her cup, blowing on the hot liquid. "They were brought into the UK on 25th January in two containers from Zeebrugge. They arrived at Tilbury Docks and were immediately driven to Birmingham."

"How do you know this?"

"We were tracking them with Europol." Pat smiled. "Maybe our last joint op before Brexit."

Amelia knew that was bollocks. Her experience with Europol was patchy at best. She doubted much would change after Brexit. There were far more pressing concerns like the immigration status and possible deportation of a number of people she knew that bothered her more.

"You said there are women and men?"

'Yes. We think they're being held at the warehouse until they pay off their passage."

Modern-day slavery.

"The men are being shipped out one at a time," Pat continued.

To babysit cannabis farms and the like. Amelia knew they would be treated as fodder. If the farms were discovered, then they would do the time rather than the gangmasters.

"And the women?" Amelia didn't know why she bothered asking. She knew their fate too.

"Nail bars and prostitution."

No surprise.

Pat added, "We picked up a woman who was shipped by the same gang to Birmingham three months ago. She was from one of the middle-income districts of China, but her family couldn't quite afford the exorbitant fees to study in the UK. The traffickers offered safe passage and the opportunity to enrol in a college, neither of which was true and the price they paid for the journey crippled both the family and her with debt that needed to be repaid."

This was a story that Amelia had heard many times.

Pat could see that Amelia was unimpressed. They both knew the score. "There was something different about this group. The woman claimed they'd get regular visits by a police official, someone who clearly had some knowledge of the local area."

Amelia sat up in her chair. "Any links to The Devil?"

"No, not him." Pat shook her head then stared at Amelia, clearly looking for signs that Amelia was still haunted by him. She was, in fact, and more importantly, so was Michal, but she didn't give anything away. "Wasn't there a police informant involved in your investigation?"

Amelia thought back to that case. "A police officer who we suspected must be high up was giving The Devil information. He was always able to evade capture. It was the only explanation. Some of the trafficked women mentioned someone, too."

"And it wasn't Branfield?"

Amelia was tempted to spit at a mention of that bastard's name. "No, we think it was someone else. The problem continued after he was banged up."

"Amelia, do you think it's someone in the NCA?"

"Possibly. But we have no evidence."

Pat whispered, "Then between you and me, we must keep each other informed of our suspicions and see if we can find the bastard who's selling us out."

"Of course." Amelia stood to leave. At the door, she turned back to her boss. "Can I ask you something?"

"Sure, hen."

"Why are you letting the lads walk all over you?"

Pat laughed. "They enjoy their little games. It keeps them where I want them, thinking they have the upper hand in a meeting. Let the kids be kids. But if one of them steps out of line on the job..."

She didn't finish the sentence — not that she needed to.

Chapter 4

Helmsmanship

Amelia and Catherine arrived at Oak Tree Training at roughly the same time. Amelia opened her car door and looked across at Catherine. The first thing she spotted was Catherine's choice of footwear: Hunter wellies. As Catherine emerged from her car, Amelia spotted a Jack Raven raincoat and a Helly Hansen polo neck. Had her partner not read the brief? They were supposed to be cleaners living on the cheap, not a pair of middle class, middle-aged boaters.

Catherine strode over and grimaced, staring at Amelia's old trainers and raincoat covered in engine oil. It was one of Joe's. He'd probably worn it fixing his classic car. Amelia had kept a few of his clothes — the ones with the best memories — and as she was tall as he had been, she wore them whenever she had the chance.

"Didn't you get the message? We're supposed to be cleaners, not retired narrowboat cruisers." Amelia asked her partner.

Catherine stroked her coat. "Oh, these. I've had these ages. I've bought some cheap stuff for tonight."

Amelia guessed that everything Catherine was wearing was actually new, and no doubt she'd treated the kids to some goodies from Go Outdoors or wherever she'd shopped the night before.

The training room was adjacent to the car park. A tall, bald man with a jovial smile greeted them with a firm handshake as they entered.

"We're just waiting for the boys, then we'll do a run-through in here of some of the parts of the boat and basic techniques."

"Thanks. I'm DI Amelia Barton and this is my colleague, DS Catherine Brown."

"Oh, we'll just stick with first names, shall we? I'll never remember all that. I'm Ted."

The "boys" arrived then. They were wearing cheap sportswear and trainers, Amelia was pleased to see.

Amelia indicated each in turn. "DS Sean Brennan and DC Amir Khan."

Sean grinned. "Yeah. We're the 'boyfriends'." He winked at Amelia, implying that his rank meant that he could nab the senior officer. Amelia ignored him. Catherine shot Amir a glance as if to say, "Just try it…"

Introductions over, Ted got underway with a short PowerPoint presentation on the parts of the boat, a few basic rope knots and a beginners' guide to locks. On the tables where they were sitting were pens and paper. Amelia wondered if she should make notes, but it seemed straightforward enough.

It wasn't long before she drifted off. Then Ted dragged her out of her stupor. "Shall we have a cuppa before heading off?"

That seemed like an excellent idea as she needed waking up. Amelia nodded in response.

As she stood by the urn, stirring her coffee, Sean sidled up next to her. "I've heard you like men of a lower rank."

Surely he couldn't be referring to Jake? Maybe he thought this was just a joke. He didn't know how lucky he was not to get covered with the boiling hot drink.

DS Jake Faris was an ex-colleague who was murdered by The Devil, but this was after he had assaulted Amelia during their short-lived relationship. Amelia knew that the different departments of the NCA were likely to gossip, but she hoped that it wasn't about her and certainly not about her poor taste in men.

At least Michal didn't fall into that category. Maybe if she mentioned his name, particularly since he was an ex-championship boxer, Sean might leave her alone. She went to open her mouth to speak when Sean suddenly blushed and muttered, "Oh shit, I've just realised... I didn't mean your dead ex…"

Now Amelia wasn't sure if he meant Joe or Jake. Instead of replying, she grabbed a biscuit and left Sean to his spluttering apology.

Tea and biscuits were soon over, and Ted ushered them outside.

The rusty, blue narrowboat named *A Cut Above* was moored right in front of them. Ted seemed happy to present it as though it was something special. "Why don't I show you around the boat first? I think you'll be pleasantly surprised."

The interior didn't match the exterior. Whoever had arranged for them to have this boat had kitted it out with some of the latest tech. The glass in the windows was tinted so that you couldn't see the cameras on tripods inside. Electrical sockets had been fitted next to the dinette, which was big enough for all four of them to sit around if necessary. There was just one double bed and that didn't look particularly long or wide. It was equipped with a matching duvet set and, although cheap, it had modern patterns of stags and rabbits. The kitchen had a serviceable cooker and fridge that someone had already stocked with an ample supply of food.

The bathroom was situated in the middle of the boat. You could lock the space for privacy by closing the doors at both sides. It held a small toilet with a modern washbasin on one side and a small shower on the other. The whole space was covered in large, plain, white tiles.

"The toilet's a cassette unit," Ted announced. Everyone looked at him blankly. "You'll have to empty it at the Elsan."

Catherine stared at him. "What do you mean — empty it?"

"There's a trolley in the cupboard by the stern. You pull out the cassette from here." Ted demonstrated what to do with the container.

Catherine looked horrified. "I'm not using that!"

Ted laughed. "Then you'll have to hold on all night. It's the only choice, I'm afraid."

The others listened to Ted explain what an Elsan was and where the nearest one was located. Catherine still appeared to be chewing a wasp.

Soon, Ted stopped talking about the boat. Gesturing back to the training room, he said, "Why don't we have some lunch then I can show you how to be a good helmsman."

Or woman. Amelia hoped that would be because she didn't think she could rely on Catherine.

Lunch consisted of sandwiches from the training centre's cafe. There wasn't much of a selection but when Amelia started on her egg and cress sandwich, she realised how hungry she was and ate it with some enthusiasm.

After a number of bites, she stopped and turned to Sean. "So how long have you been working for the NCA?"

"Two years, mostly with the Modern Slavery Unit. You've mostly done sex work, haven't you?" Sean seemed to be enjoying his sandwich as he took a huge bite.

"Not exactly." It wasn't like she undertook it herself, for fuck's sake. "Sex trafficking isn't work. It's human slavery in its most obscene and abusive form."

They were both on the same side, working for the same unit, only Amelia had chosen to concentrate on cases involving sex trafficking. Her managers hadn't stopped her as yet but, more and more, the lines blurred across each unit in the NCA as more and more traffickers exploited people in all types of slavery, drug running and prostitution. If they didn't specialise, then neither could Amelia, so the fact that this case crossed the boundaries had not come as a shock. She would just have to try to work in a team that she was never comfortable with.

Ted stood up. "Shall we go and move this boat, then?"

The plan was to cruise the boat to Fazeley Junction then move it in the morning to the chosen mooring opposite the factory.

Catherine didn't appear to hear him. She was hunched over her phone, frowning. *What's up with her? She seems so distracted lately,* Amelia thought.

Amelia strode over to her partner and tapped her on the shoulder. She felt her physically jump before putting her phone in her pocket and zipping it shut.

"Sorry. Is it time to go?"

"Yeah. You ready?" Catherine followed

Amelia out of the door and onto the stern of the boat.

Ted showed them all how to start the engine. "Check the control's in neutral. See, when I turn the key, this yellow light comes on. Well, hold the key in that position for about twenty seconds before fully turning it." The boat rumbled into life.

The men unhooked the ropes from the rings and Sean cast off, pushing the front end of the boat away from the towpath. That part went relatively smoothly.

With everyone on board, the stern was crowded. Ted said, "Tell you what, lads. Why don't you get the kettle on and I'll introduce the ladies to steering the boat."

Ladies. Amelia glanced at Catherine and raised her eyebrows. At least Ted hadn't sent them to make the tea.

Catherine took the tiller first, making it look easy. She seemed to be able to keep the boat in a straight line at least. Then it was Amelia's turn. As soon as she took over, the boat seemed to have a will of its own, heading straight for the far bank.

Ted guided the tiller towards the bank, which seemed ludicrous to Amelia. "Just point the tiller at the bank you want to miss, not head towards."

Amelia had another go and, although she still zig-zagged across the cut, they made some progress. Catherine took over as they approached a bridge. "What if a boat comes the other way?"

Ted smiled. "Just judge who's nearer to the bridge. It's pretty much first come, first served."

"How do you stop the bloody thing?!" Amelia knew she had a point — the boat must weigh a good few tons.

Ted just grinned that daft grin again. "Ease off the throttle and if you need to slow down more quickly then give it a bit of reverse."

The men appeared a few moments later with their drink orders.

"Our turn, I believe." Sean took over the tiller.

Amelia and Catherine stepped down into the cabin with their drinks and settled at the dinette. A few moments later, there was the distinct sound of scraping and their drinks slopped onto the table.

"They might need a little more practise than us," Amelia observed, rescuing her coffee.

But Catherine wasn't listening. She was back on her phone.

Amelia sighed and looked out of the window. At least they were going in the right direction. A family of ducks glided past, or at least mum and a trail of ducklings. It wasn't long before she began to relax, an unusual feeling for Amelia, who would start getting restless a few seconds after sitting down on any normal day.

Catherine fired off another text. As she glanced out of the window, Amelia could see that she was crying.

For a moment, Amelia didn't know what to say. They had a purely work relationship. She coughed and said, "Look, I don't know what's going on, but there's clearly something amiss. A problem…?"

She stopped herself from ending the sentence. It made her sound like her mother.

"I'm okay." Catherine wiped her face with her coat sleeve.

"Really?" Amelia couldn't just stay silent. *Leave it alone.*

"It's just my niece. She's in a bit of a mess."

"What sort of mess?"

Catherine sighed. "Drug dealing sort of mess. Or, at least, that's what my sister thinks."

"Why?"

"Sorry?"

"Why does your sister think your niece is dealing?"

Catherine placed her phone down on the table. It immediately began to vibrate and light up again.

Instead of picking it up, Catherine continued. "Aleesha, my niece, goes away for days. Doesn't tell anyone where she's going or where she's been."

"Maybe she's just got a boyfriend? How old is she?"

"Sixteen. Just."

"So it's not illegal, then." Not that it seemed to stop most people; it certainly hadn't stopped her.

"She's got money too... new clothes..."

Why was it that every time anyone mentioned money and clothes to Amelia, her immediate thought was child sexual exploitation, not drugs?

"How is she when she gets back?"

"Rude, sullen. Won't talk about where she's been." Catherine bit her lip.

"I've got a teenager. Sounds fairly typical behaviour to me." Becky had her moments, but Amelia knew that she was lucky compared to the anxiety some parents went through with their offspring.

"Marsha, my sister, found some train

tickets in Aleesha's coat."

Amelia sat up. "For where?"

"Places near Oxford and Reading. Smaller town stations."

"Has she got friends who've recently moved there?" Amelia knew this was clutching at straws. The gangs moved their mules around to different towns to sell and deliver drugs. They had enough fodder in the cities. The smaller towns in the counties and shires, seaside resorts and large villages were where they could make money now. Kids like Aleesha were expendable across county lines.

"I'll ask my sister about any friends, but I doubt it. Alarm bells are ringing. You can imagine why but what do I say to my sister? That her suspicions are likely to be true?"

"Would she report her? Most parents won't. That's the problem. They don't want the authorities involved."

"No. Never." Catherine stared at Amelia. "Would you report Becky?"

Not report her, no. But lock her up for a few years? Maybe.

Before Amelia could think of a believable response, Sean hollered through the boat, "We're here."

They'd decided to moor up before they reached the locks in the centre of the city. What they didn't want was to arrive without being prepared. They had to look the part from the outset.

Tomorrow, they'd spend the morning travelling to the spot opposite the abandoned factory.

Amelia guessed she'd be spending the evening rehearsing her new identity and making sure she packed suitable clothing. She wondered if the others would be so diligent.

Chapter 5

Locking Down

Amelia regularly drove to Birmingham on the M6. She had thought she knew Spaghetti Junction, but there was a world beneath. Concrete towers held up the road as the canal towpath widened. Amelia sat in the bow of the boat on a plank covered in pretty cushions. They'd been travelling for a few hours and now had to make their first big decision: which turn did they need to take at the junction?

Ted had left them a canal planner, a route marked on a map that showed the locks and bridges. The Birmingham and Fazeley swung to the left, while going straight on would move them away from Birmingham. Amelia was tempted to suggest that they take that route instead, away from the grime and dirt of the city.

The calmness that she had experienced yesterday returned as soon as she stepped on the narrowboat, all stress gone, channelled into the water. For a brief moment, she wondered if she should suggest to her family that they should get a boat but, like the wave from the bow, it soon rippled away to nothing.

A small group of lads weaved on their bikes around the graffiti-covered columns. One of them shouted, "Oi, Granny! What ya staring at, ya dumb fuck?"

They were still in Brum. Amelia sighed and headed to the stern to make sure Catherine knew which fork to take. A wrong turn now would cost them valuable time. As she stepped through the cabin, she tried to avoid bumping her head on the ceiling and bumping into the walls. There were times when her height was a disadvantage. The lads were playing cards in the dinette, a few coins on the table. A pot to win, no doubt. Amelia couldn't be bothered to order them to stop since they'd reach the locks shortly and they would need to lend a hand.

Catherine had read the sign pointing to the canal route they needed to take and was already steering the boat that way.

"You really are a natural," Amelia muttered.

Catherine leant closer. "Sorry, you'll have to speak up. I can't hear you over the sound of the engine."

"Never mind." Amelia noticed that her colleague appeared far less distracted today. When she got the chance, she'd ask her if she'd spoken to her sister about avenues to consider.

They weren't far from the first lock. Amelia sounded the horn using the small button in front of the engine throttle. It made a deep, penetrating noise. Sean and Amir came bounding out the boat like two young puppies.

"What the hell was that?" Sean asked.

"We're at the locks. You'd better get the windlasses out. You're on."

They might as well work the locks. Catherine could stay on the tiller as she seemed to be the best at manoeuvring the boat. If Amelia helped her, then she'd be able to chat to her about her niece.

Sean had other ideas. "We've got three windlasses. Why don't me and Amir work this one and you can get the next one ready."

He handed Amelia the rustiest windlass. She swapped it for the shiny one in his hand. When he grimaced at her, she stepped off the boat onto the towpath, ignoring him.

It was only when she reached the second lock that Amelia realised that she'd forgotten everything Ted had told them the day before. The water was not level. It was higher inside the lock than in front of it. Amelia realised that she had to somehow get the water out of the lock. She was walking up the steps next to the second lock when a middle-aged woman with a windlass in her belt came striding towards her.

She'd left a man, who Amelia guessed was her husband, at the tiller of their shorter boat, which was approaching the lock from the opposite direction.

"Hi," shouted the woman, "shall we buddy up?"

If Amelia had to guess, then she'd have put this woman down as a retired teacher. She had that tone about her. Amelia decided it was best to come clean and have a tutorial.

"This is my first lock," she admitted.

The woman started pushing the lock gate open with her bottom. "They're easy enough with practice."

Her husband steered the boat neatly between the sides of the lock and she pushed the lock gate shut.

"Come with me." She nudged Amelia. She strode over to the other gate and placed the square hole in the windlass over the spindle. "You just turn this and the paddles open."

As she turned, Amelia heard the sudden whoosh of water. The water in the lock was draining out and the boat lowered with it.

"Keep going until you can't turn the spindle any further." The woman stopped turning and took the windlass off the spindle. "Top tip: never leave the windlass on the spindle or it's likely to fly off and hit you on the head."

Amelia smiled.

"Why don't you do the other paddle?" The woman gestured to the other side of the gate. "You can walk across the top of the gate."

The water had dropped a great deal, leaving quite a gap between the top of the gate and the canal. Amelia gingerly stepped onto the board with one hand on the rusty, white rail that ran along the top of the gate. Two long strides and she was on the other side, ready to open the paddle.

Sean and Amir had just started to shut the gates of their first lock when the woman shouted, "Leave it open. We're coming through."

Catherine steered their narrowboat towards the side and cut the engine, waiting for the woman's husband to steer their boat out of the lock.

They all soon got into a routine. Amelia relaxed, surprised at the industrial beauty of the canal. It seemed to be a hidden world that even travelled beneath some of the larger factories and commercial buildings of the city centre.

It wasn't long before they reached their destination. Mooring up required attaching some chains to the metal bars that ran along the edge of the canal. Sean seemed to have mastered tight knots, so Amelia left him to it. Instead, she walked the towpath, glancing casually over at their target.

The red-brick factory dominated the local landscape. Its shattered windows made it appear broken and crying. Amelia shuddered, knowing that was what its occupants were experiencing and feeling.

She returned to the boat. Catherine had

put the kettle on and Sean was setting up the surveillance equipment in the back of the boat. The beds had been removed from this berth in order to fit the laptops and cameras on tripods in. The window had special electrochromic glass fitted, which meant that they wouldn't be seen by anyone on the opposite towpath even with the lights on. When they weren't working in the cabin, they could let the light back in with a flick of a switch.

Catherine opened the fridge. "We're running low on milk."

A great opportunity to get Catherine on her own, Amelia thought. "Why don't we find a local shop while the lads finish setting up the equipment?"

"Good idea," Catherine smiled. "We can drink these first then set off."

Amelia took her phone out of her pocket and fired up Google maps. "Looks like there's a small supermarket not too far from here, about a ten-minute walk."

Amir appeared then and grabbed his cup of tea. "If you want, I can cook us a curry tonight."

"That's a lovely idea. Why don't you go to the shop with Amelia and pick up the ingredients?" Catherine nodded towards her colleague.

Amelia grimaced; she'd have to think of another plan to get Catherine on her own.

"Sure, that's fine."

Amir opened one of the kitchen cupboards. "We seem to have lots of good-quality pans, so we should be able to cook here."

Ted had made sure they had two full gas bottles, which should last them a while. The team had prepared the boat well. It seemed surveillance from a boat wasn't going to be so much of a challenge after all.

Amelia scrutinised Amir as they made their way to the local corner shop. She'd assumed he was in his twenties and very much a rookie but, on closer inspection, he was more likely to be in his mid-thirties. His jet-black hair showed signs of grey, and he had the beginnings of crow's feet at the corners of his eyes. His skin was flawless, making Amelia wonder if he moisturised.

She'd never been attracted to that type of man, much preferring the more conventional, stereotypical strong guy who wouldn't be seen dead using skin-care products or even consider hair care, apart from, maybe, Jake. Thinking about it, he probably was vain enough to buy and use expensive beauty products.

Amir must have decided that he needed to make conversation. "Have you been in the force long?"

Seriously? Amelia yawned. "Since I was twenty-one."

Amir nodded and stared at the ground. This wasn't going well.

After a few awkward minutes, Amelia asked, "How many years have you been a DC?" *Let's see just how much of a rookie you are.*

"This is my second year. I've only been in the NCA six months, though. I was based in Wolverhampton before that."

A young woman strode towards them wearing her coat wrapped tightly around her. She could be Chinese or Vietnamese, Amelia couldn't tell from a distance, but she was stick-thin — painfully thin, even. The bag of shopping in her hand appeared to be heavier than she was.

Amelia strode up to her. "Hi. We're just moored up on the canal. Where's the nearest shop where we can buy bread and milk?"

The woman shrank back, pulling the bag closer to her, shaking her head.

"Sorry." Amelia repeated her question, slowly this time.

But the woman didn't answer. She continued shaking her head as she pushed past Amelia and scuttled away in the direction of the boat.

Amir caught her up. "Do you think...?"

"That she's one of the women from the factory?" Amelia paused. "Yes, probably."

"Vietnamese?"

"Certainly, that area."

Once Amelia had seen her closer, if she was to hazard a guess, then it was likely that she was from Southeast Asia. Facially, she had delicate features and beautiful, wide eyes, but she had the gauntness associated with malnourishment. The bastards were, no doubt, not feeding the women properly even if they trusted them to move around the local area on their own.

The local shop had all the ingredients that Amir needed for his curry. The bags provided by the store were paper thin and Amelia feared they'd lose the fresh coriander, tins of coconut milk and the rest of the shopping before they reached the boat. She had visions of chasing down the towpath for an errant onion.

Back at the boat, Amir settled into the kitchen to prepare the curry. Sean was sipping from a can of lager while fiddling with one of the cameras. Amelia and Catherine left them to it.

The plan was for them all to stay on the boat that night and settle in. What this actually meant was that they could discuss the rota and their cover stories, ensure that all the equipment was working and, during the night, see if they could spot anywhere around the factory to set up small cameras or microphones. Tonight, they might only have a recce. The worst thing that could happen would be for them to be discovered snooping by the gangmasters.

Catherine sat opposite Amelia and opened the case files on her laptop. Amelia hoped to have a chat with her about her niece, but Catherine clearly wanted to concentrate on work. Amelia didn't blame her. That's what she did, too, when her personal life became difficult.

"Did Amir mention that we might have made contact with one of the captive women?"

Catherine stopped scrolling and glanced over to Amelia. "No, he didn't. Was this while you were out?"

"Yes. I spoke to her, but she couldn't get away from me fast enough."

"Do you think she was being watched?"

Amelia considered this. It was possible and would explain her terror. "Oh, God. Do you think I've got her in trouble?"

"I wouldn't have thought so if she didn't speak."

Amelia's phone vibrated next to her. Pat's name came up on the display.

"Hi, boss."

Pat tutted. "Don't bother with that. Listen, I'd like you and Catherine to investigate a local nail bar in the morning. See if you can get your nails done. It's possible they're using women from the factory."

"Sure. You got the address?"

Amelia scrawled it down on the back of a

receipt she had in her pocket.

Then Pat cut the call without any pleasantries.

"Okay?" Catherine asked.

Amelia filled her in. Glancing down at her hands, she wondered what the girls in the nail bar would make of her uneven and rarely painted nails. Maybe they'd charge her double for all the effort it would need to improve them? Catherine, of course, had subtly painted nails, all perfectly manicured and in perfect proportion.

Chapter 6

The Undertaker

The Undertaker hated these jobs, emptying trucks of their aborted cargo and cleansing them of their deceased load.

He opened the back of the truck with the keys that had been posted through his letterbox. Only one body today. It could have been far worse. He placed his backpack inside and then pulled himself up into the truck.

The body of a teenage boy was crouched at the far end of the truck, chin down on his chest. He could have been asleep. The Undertaker knew it would be a painful extraction. Rigor mortis had set in, making it difficult to transfer the body to a body bag. He rolled him over, noticing that he'd soiled his trousers. More fluids to clean up when he'd done.

After some forceful tugging and stretching of plastic, The Undertaker rolled the bag to the open door and dropped it onto the tarmac below. He would transfer it to his van later, but he now had to clean up. No traces must be found of the nameless migrant or the others that had found freedom — or enslavement, whichever way you saw it. He didn't care. He was just employed as a fixer.

Chapter 7

The Nail Bar

The sleeping arrangements were causing some strife. The back bunks had been removed to accommodate all their surveillance equipment. The plan was that they wouldn't all need to stay together on the boat often. The women would supposedly be at their cleaning jobs during the day but, having been on watch all night, would actually be sleeping at home, while the men would supposedly return from their night-time security jobs each morning and would be on watch all day. However, they needed some time to prepare so that evening found them all looking for somewhere to sleep.

There was a three-quarter size double bed, the only other option being the dinette.

"Do you think the table comes down to make a double like in a caravan?" Catherine looked under it to see if there was a mechanism.

"I can't see any way of making a mattress. Can you?" Amelia stood up, wrenched up the seat she'd been sitting on and found a few folded blankets. "Try your side."

Catherine stood up and did the same, only to find a few rusting tools.

"The lads can share the bed. You'll probably be able to lie across the dinette seat."

Catherine looked her colleague up and down. "And what will you do?" There was no way Amelia's six-foot frame would fit on the dinette bench.

"I'll stay awake. I've got plenty of work to do and, besides, we're going over to the factory later tonight, so we won't be getting much sleep anyway."

"And the nail bar tomorrow?"

"If we book in the morning for the early afternoon, I can get some sleep at home." She would be able to see Callum, if not her girls.

"Sounds like a plan. I'll go and tell the lads they're sharing."

Amir's curry was a roaring success. He'd clearly had a lot of practice. The level of spiciness seemed to suit everyone. Fortunately, everyone ate meat as the main dish was a creamy lamb bhuna.

Amelia stayed awake, nibbling on leftover naan bread and writing notes in the case file. Catherine slept opposite her, gently snoring. They'd set alarms for 3 am. Hopefully, the brothel would be shut for the night by then. It was a weeknight, after all.

As she typed, Amelia noticed the drop in temperature. The narrowboat had been warm enough during the day but she stood up and fetched a blanket from under the seat, then shut her laptop and let her thoughts drift.

This was always dangerous. A darkening sense of dread always sat inches away. Amelia could block it out when she was busy, but not when she relaxed. It grabbed her then. If she had seen a counsellor, they would have told her that she had PTSD. Over the past few years, Amelia's recurrent traumas had never been fully resolved. Instead, she pushed them away, only for them to resurface in nightmares or as panic attacks.

Michal had helped but he was dealing with his own traumas now.

It took a while, but she dozed off eventually, only to be woken by the alarm minutes later. Catherine heard it, too.

Stretching, she sat up, a calm, relaxed smile on her face. "Shall I get the kettle on?"

Amelia grunted in reply. Sean walked in, wearing only his boxers and an Aston Villa football shirt. Amelia turned away from him.

"Thought I'd get the kettle on but I see you've already done it. Didn't get much sleep — that Amir tosses and turns all night." He cracked his fingers. "Be good to get to work though, eh?"

It certainly would. The narrowboat seemed to shrink in size with everyone moving about and Amelia felt distinctly claustrophobic. She pulled on her trainers. "Is the gear ready in the bags?"

Sean nodded. "Prepared it this afternoon."

"Get dressed. As soon as we've drunk this, we'll get off."

The towpath was difficult to make out in the darkness. They could not use torches, so had to rely on their night vision. It took a few seconds to adjust to the gloom, but they did not have far to go.

About a hundred metres down the towpath was a lock, which meant they could cross to the other side. Amelia judged that it was not worth risking an accident so took an adjustable torch out of her pocket. Changing its setting to a lower one, the beam just about allowed her to see the wooden lock gate and the white metal bar on top. She crossed safely. Shining her torch for the others, they too were able to traverse the lock.

The plan was for Amelia and Catherine to keep watch on the metal fire escape and the street surrounding the warehouse. Sean would drill holes in the brickwork to enable Amir to place the tech. Their tiny cameras and listening devices would slide easily into the wall.

First, Amir and Sean had to snip back the wire that led to the back of the building along the narrow edge of the canal. The ground was still muddy from the previous night's rain. Amir's boot slipped on the thin strip of grass and mud separating the building from the edge of the canal, and he was lucky not to fall in or catch himself on the barbed wire. He trod more gingerly after that.

Catherine appeared distracted, only watching the guys for a few seconds at a time before drifting off. Amelia nudged her. "Stay focussed. We'll need to signal the lads if anyone leaves or arrives at the factory."

"Sorry," Catherine muttered.

No one arrived or left, and the surveillance gear was installed without a hitch.

Back at the narrowboat, Amir fired up the laptops. It took a while for the signal to load. The picture quality was not great — grainy at best, the colours muted. He pressed a few keys and the picture marginally improved.

He muttered, "I'll have another go in the morning, but this could be the best that we can get. The camera's not that sophisticated."

Inside the factory walls, on the ground floor, mattresses littered the floor. There had been an attempt to partition the large area with plastic clothes airers. These were arranged to offer a small amount of privacy to each of the beds.

A group of women slept in one corner, mostly facing away from the camera, their bodies covered with small, checked cotton sheets. At least it was springtime. In winter, they'd freeze.

One woman sat at the foot of her mattress with her head in her hands. Amelia wondered if she was weeping. A group of four stocky men were playing cards, each sitting on a mattress, the floor between them forming a makeshift table. They chewed matchsticks, which they also used as gambling chips. One of them started to cough and spat his matchstick out, only helping himself to a new one a couple of seconds later. It struck Amelia that here was a scene involving adults that did not have anyone scrolling through a phone or tablet. It could have been ten years ago. It seemed so unnatural today.

"How many do you think there are?" Sean appeared to be trying to count them.

"At least twenty here. But this is only one floor."

The factory had three further floors. They had not risked using ladders in order to view the other floors. There was no room to lean them up against the back wall of the factory anyway. "Make a note and short description of each person we can see."

Sean nodded. He reached for a pad and started writing in it. Catherine opened another of the laptops. "When you've done that, Sean, I'll add them to our case notes."

They continued like this for a couple of hours until Amir stretched. "Who's for breakfast?"

Amelia had the faces of the factory occupants etched in her brain as she walked with Catherine from the narrowboat to the nail bar. There weren't many women visible in the factory, so she didn't expect to recognise any one of them at the salon.

It must have been nail rush hour. The place was rammed, each of the nail stylists at a workbench with a client seated opposite. Amelia counted eight of them in the tiny space. Not one of them spoke other than to ask the client which polish and style they wanted.

As Amelia and Catherine entered the shop, the receptionist, who appeared older and more stern than the stylists, thrust a catalogue into their hands. "Choose from here. It'll be 'bout half hour."

There were numbers next to each style and a fixed price. It could have been a Chinese takeaway rather than a nail boutique. Amelia hadn't been in a nail bar before and she rarely entered a hairdressing salon, having neither the time nor inclination. Catherine must be a regular, Amelia thought, with her manicured talons.

"Is this normal?"

Catherine took a seat and waited for her boss to sit down next to her. "Not really. The place I go in the city centre's more like an upmarket hair salon. Lots of chat about holidays and free coffee."

I wouldn't want to drink coffee made here. They might well use canal water.

Catherine continued. "It's cheap, though. I mean, really cheap."

That must be its appeal because Amelia couldn't see why anyone would enter the salon otherwise.

Leaning in again, Catherine said, "I have to say, though, they're quite talented. I've seen much worse handiwork." She nodded as one of the clients admired her nails as she left.

It was soon Amelia's turn. She chose number five, a basic manicure and polish. The stylist didn't look up to meet her eyes when she told her. Amelia noticed they were a soft brown above the pale blue face mask that she wore. Instead, she took her right hand in hers. Stretching out her fingers, checking the nails, she sighed and pulled the face mask down below her chin with her other hand. "Not been before?"

Amelia grinned. "That obvious?"

"Yeah." The young stylist didn't smile, just pulled up her face mask and reached for her file.

"Haven't I seen you before? Me and my friend have got a narrowboat. Do you live near the canal?"

The girl started filing and shrugged. "All us Vietnamese look the same, huh?"

"Sorry. I didn't mean that." Amelia found it hard to keep her hand still. "You don't live over that way, then."

"No." The girl glanced over at the receptionist. Amelia sensed that she needed to stop asking questions while she was under the madam's glare. Yes, that was it. A brothel madam, that's what the older woman reminded her of.

The receptionist walked past then, glared at her and asked, "Everything okay?"

"Fine. She's doing a lovely job." The woman walked off, checking the handiwork of the other girls as she went. Amelia hoped Catherine was having more luck.

Perhaps if she just chatted, she might get her stylist to open up more. "Have you been in the UK long? The weather's horrible, isn't it?"

"Always wet. Just like my hometown."

"Your hometown?"

The girl glared at her. "You know Vietnam?"

"No. Not really."

"Then why does it matter where I'm from?"

Amelia shrugged. "Just making conversation. What's your name by the way? I'm Amelia."

"Teri."

Really? How likely was that?

Teri let go of her hand and gestured for the other one. "You need to take better care of your nails. There's nothing to file."

As if to prove this, she grazed the tip of her finger with the nail file.

"Ouch." Amelia instinctively pulled her hand away.

Teri's eyes grew wide as she glanced towards her supervisor. Fortunately, the elder woman hadn't heard. But the fear was tangible.

"Sorry."

"It's okay. My fault. I shouldn't bite them." Amelia gave Teri her hand back.

She waited to pounce. Once the girl had regained her composure, Amelia whispered, bowing her head nearer Teri's, "We can get you out, you know."

"What do you mean?"

"You don't have to stay here. If you need help —"

Teri grabbed the natural-coloured polish. Skilfully, she applied it to the first fingernail. "You shouldn't believe everything you read." Amelia raised her eyebrows. "Not all Vietnamese women are slaves."

Next time, Amelia thought, *say it like you mean it.*

It wasn't long before her nail transformation was complete. It looked far better than when she'd walked in, even Amelia had to admit that.

The sour-faced receptionist took her

money. "That's £5.70."

Amelia took her debit card out of her pocket.

The woman pointed to a small, yellowing sign in the window. "Cash only. No cards."

Catherine called over, "Don't worry. I'll pay for us both. I have cash."

Who didn't take cards these days?

An hour later Catherine and Amelia were sitting in Pat's office back at WMROC. So much for getting a rest before the night shift on the boat. At least Pat provided a good strong coffee.

"Well? How did it go at the nail bar?"

"Don't know for sure, but it seems likely that the girls there have a minder." Amelia got out her phone. She scrolled until she reached a photo that she'd taken. "I'll forward you a photo of the receptionist-come-jailer. Let us know if you pick anything up from face recognition."

Pat opened her laptop. After a few keyboard clicks, she said, "Got it. Thanks." Then she looked back at her team. "First impressions?"

"The girls weren't very forthcoming and not very chatty. The salon only takes cash, and the charges are nominal." Catherine had pocketed a brochure and handed it to Pat.

"Money laundering?"

"A possibility." Amelia stretched; her muscles ached from not getting any proper rest. "I'm not sure how, though."

"Cash regularly changes hands there. They could easily be moving money away from the main sex business or other less legitimate work."

"Guess so."

"Check out the company records, if there are any. It could be they're just not paying any tax, so nothing goes through the books. They might just open in empty shops and keep moving on. We just happened to notice that there was a nail bar near the factory and put two-and-two together." Pat glanced over at Amelia. "Go home and get some sleep. You're on duty this evening. What time are you due back on the boat?"

Amelia glanced at her phone. "In about three-and-a-half hours."

"It's amazing what you can do on three hours' sleep." Pat shut her laptop. They'd been dismissed.

As they left the office, Amelia turned to Catherine. "How's your niece?"

"Not good. She went missing again last night."

That explained why she'd been distracted. "Have they found her yet?"

"No. No, they haven't." Catherine glanced down at her phone as though expecting it to ring.

"Why don't we speak to one of the county lines specialists? They might know where she could be."

Amelia knew a detective who could help. He wasn't based at WMROC. He had an office in one of the nearby stations.

"No." Catherine did not look at her partner. "We can do that tomorrow if she doesn't show up." Then Catherine put her phone away. "I've got to get home."

Amelia watched her almost break into a run on the way to her car. Amelia guessed she'd be the same if it was one of her girls, with the family expecting that she could solve anything even though she'd be just as useless as the rest of them.

Chapter 8

County Lines

The night shift passed slowly. Throughout the night, rain hammered on the roof of the narrowboat, reminding Amelia of childhood caravan holidays in Skegness. Her aunt would encourage her to play cards with her cousins when all she wanted to do was swim in the sea. One year, the rain belted down all week. Arguments stormed and raged in the confined space but anything was better than being stuck at home with her alcoholic mother.

Catherine spent the night concentrating on the comings and goings at the factory. Even when it was clear that the punters had all gone home and the clattering on the metal fire escape staircase on the side of the factory had ended, she still stared at the computer screen.

Amelia left her to it. She'd received the case notes and post-mortem report on the recently discovered female corpse. She picked up the canal map and guidebook left by the helmsmanship trainer. With a sharpie, she marked the factory where the woman's body had been found. It was easily walkable from where they were moored. What was it with Birmingham's industrial past that made it such a hotbed of modern slavery?

Amelia sighed and turned back to the report on the body. The woman's arm had been amputated post-mortem. The slender arm and tiny hand tipped with bright red nail polish were covered in rat bites. The rose tattoo had been photographed and was an exact match for that found on one of the other murdered women. The same brand. No doubt, the same tattooist.

Amelia wondered if they'd been marched off to a local artist or whether the branding was done by one of their jailers. The other tattoos were all roses but in different styles and different locations on the body, so maybe it was the former. Amelia made a reference to this in the case notes. Perhaps the young detective on the case would follow it up with local tattoo parlours.

An hour later, there was a loud knock on the well deck doors. It was Amir and Sean announcing their return from their "security jobs". They'd brought back pastries with them from the bakery in the local market. There'd be just enough time for breakfast before leaving with Catherine for their "day jobs".

When Catherine joined them at the dinette, Amir gestured towards the factory. "Anything happen I should know about?"

He had to wait for an answer as Catherine was stuck into the Danish. Between mouthfuls, he got a brief, "Nothing much, it's all in the notes."

"What's the plan for today?" Amelia still felt that the women had drawn the short straw.

"I thought we might follow anyone who leaves the factory to see if we can get a positive link with the nail bar," Sean smiled.

"Makes sense," Amelia paused, "But I wouldn't leave the factory for too long. We haven't seen any of the main players yet."

The only gangmasters they'd seen up to now were foot-soldiers. Amelia was convinced of that.

"So, what are you two ladies up to today?" Amir grinned.

Amelia and Catherine raised eyebrows in unison.

"*Ladies?*" Amelia spluttered.

Amir blushed. "Sorry, I meant —"

"Too late." Catherine took a cinnamon whirl out of the paper bag and took a bite.

"Tut, tut, Amir. You've gone right down in my estimation." Amelia stood up and grabbed her rucksack. "Time to go."

Catherine wiped her hands on her jeans and followed her boss to the stern doors. Before they climbed the steps up to the deck, Amelia asked, "Are you still okay to go to meet Dominic?"

"Dominic?"

"The DI in West Mids who specialises in county lines." Amelia pushed the hatch back, climbed the steps and opened the doors to the stern deck.

Catherine followed her along the towpath. "Yeah. I suppose so. Is he based in Brum?"

"Just down the road, as it happens."

DI Dominic Starley could have been any age. He wore black jeans and a black hoodie rather than the customary shirt and trousers, albeit without a tie. No one seemed to bother with those anymore or with doing up the top button of their shirts. It didn't bother Amelia, but Catherine seemed surprised at his casual look.

When he smiled, which he appeared to do a lot, he looked even younger. He'd trained with Amelia, so he wasn't kidding her. The greying hair at his temples told their own story, too.

Having introduced Catherine and given Dominic a brief rundown of what the issue was, Amelia asked directly, "So do you think she could be involved in county lines? And what can we do about it?"

Dominic, who was sitting on the only

table in the small meeting room, turned towards Catherine. "What do you think? Could she be involved in smuggling drugs?'

"Yes... I mean, it seems the only logical explanation." Catherine bit her lip. "She's gone missing so many times. When she comes home, she's so vile to everyone that no one wants to ask her where she's been or what she's been up to. It's easier, I guess, to leave her be than confront her. I'm not sure? Should we have it out with her?"

Dominic shrugged. "You could do, but my guess is that she'd just run again or give you a mouthful of abuse."

"She can't enjoy what she's doing, surely." Catherine took out her mobile and stared at the screen.

"'Enjoy' is probably not the right word. But she's getting something from it. New clothes, money, independence. Mind you, if she tries to leave the gang, then they'll make things difficult for her."

"In what way?" Amelia stared at Dominic, waiting for an answer. She could only imagine what Catherine was going through. It could easily be Becky in this situation.

"Threaten to tell her family, maybe even harm them."

Not that much different to what they found with sex trafficking and CSEA, then. This was just another form of grooming and abuse of young people.

He continued. "It's not easy to be a girl in a gang. The lads might be at more risk of violence, but the girls are often used as bait to lure gang members from other areas to a location where they can be sheffed - stabbed. They're also passed around for sex."

Catherine visibly shivered.

Dominic turned back to her. "Can I show you some photographs of known gang members and drug runners?"

"Sure. Not that I'd necessarily know who my niece was hanging around with."

DI Starley stood up and reached for his laptop. He opened up the screen and typed a few words before handing the laptop to Catherine. She stared at the screen and clicked occasionally to move on to the next set of photographs.

After a few minutes, she stopped and glanced up. She turned the laptop around to face Amelia and Dominic, pointing at a photograph. "That's her. That's my niece."

Dominic took the laptop from her. "Aleesha Coleman is your niece?"

"Yes. You know her, then?"

Dominic sighed. "Yeah, we've picked her up a couple of times."

"You've *arrested* her?" Catherine scowled. Amelia wondered why she was getting angry.

"Not exactly." Dominic put the laptop back on the table. "We reported her to Social Services. Your sister knows this."

Catherine stared at the floor. "She never said."

Amelia stroked her colleague's arm. "She probably didn't want to tell you. Pride, maybe... or maybe she thought it'd get you into trouble."

Catherine stood up. "I'm sorry I've wasted your time."

Dominic also stood up. "You haven't. Listen, Aleesha's known to us and is at risk. We need to know when she's not at home."

The look that Catherine gave would have soured milk. "Why? So you can arrest her again?"

Dominic didn't seem bothered by it. "No, so we can help find her."

Amelia wasn't sure if she should intervene. Aleesha was clearly still missing or why would Catherine be checking her phone every couple of minutes? But it was not her place to say.

Catherine sighed. "She's been gone for a week, ten days at most. I don't think my sister's told anyone."

"I'll have to let Aleesha's social worker know." Dominic took his phone out of his jeans pocket.

"She's sixteen. Why would they be interested?" This wasn't what Amelia had expected from Catherine, who was being offered help. She wondered if she'd done the right thing bringing Catherine here. "Look, I shouldn't be here. My sister won't thank me for it. If you find her, then great, but maybe this should stay as family business."

Catherine shot a look of disdain at Amelia as though it was her fault that she was here and marched out of the meeting room.

Amelia didn't follow her.

Dominic sat down again and folded his arms. "Aleesha's pretty entrenched in RB7."

"But that's a Coventry gang. I assumed from Catherine that she lived in Birmingham."

"Maybe she hooked up with a lad in Hillfields. Or maybe Catherine lives in Brum but her sister doesn't."

Dominic opened his laptop again and searched for a grime video on YouTube. It showed lads wearing RB7 colours sitting on the bonnet of a car. Aleesha could be seen dancing against the car with a couple of other girls the same age. They were grinding away and posing for the camera. She looked younger than sixteen.

Amelia asked, "When was this?"

"About two years ago."

"Shit."

"Yep." Dominic stood. Amelia noticed how tall he was. He smiled then and said, "Sorry to be the bringer of bad news."

"It's not your fault."

"Glad you think so." He blushed. "I don't suppose you've got some time for a drink in the near future?"

"Time... what's that?"

"Yeah, I know." He sucked his teeth. "But surely a bit of cross-cooperation would be good for our departments?"

He was being an absolute flirt but, for some reason, Amelia wasn't put off by it. Maybe she was missing male company. It wasn't as though Michal could complain as she'd barely seen him.

She took a card out of a side pocket in her bag and handed it to him. "Just in case we need to collaborate, you've got my number."

When Amelia arrived home, she wasn't surprised to find that everyone had gone out. The girls would be at school, Jola had probably taken Callum to the park or shopping and her mum had her craft club. There was a meal in the fridge that just needed heating up. Usually, Amelia would work for a while before hitting the sack, but today all she wanted to do was wolf down the chilli, have a shower and hit the sack.

Of course, her job had other ideas. She'd only eaten two forkfuls when her mobile rang. It was Dominic.

She was about to tell him that he was being a tad over keen when he said, "Sorry, you must be knackered. There's been a sighting of Aleesha at New Street with a couple of much younger kids in tow. I thought you'd want to let your partner know."

Amelia thanked him and immediately rang Catherine. She sounded as sleepy as Amelia felt. Amelia was starting to think that she shouldn't have let herself get roped into this whole mess. She conveyed Dominic's message and waited.

Catherine didn't answer straight away. Maybe she was still smarting from earlier. "New Street, did you say?"

"Yes."

"She'll be long gone by now." Another long pause. "Do you think DI Starley could get the CCTV? Maybe we could find out which train she got on."

Catherine was right. Neither she nor Amelia could have a valid procedural reason to ask for the tape, but Dom could request it. "Why don't we see if we can meet him at the station, then at least we won't have to wait for him to get back to us."

"Good idea." She sighed. "Thanks, Amelia. I really appreciate this."

So much for a good day's sleep.

New Street Station might have been recently refurbished, but Amelia always thought that it looked incomplete. The inner parade of shops always seemed busy but people waiting on the platforms looked uncomfortable. The passage from the trains to the concourse added a new element of claustrophobia and the rush to the escalators was downright dangerous. Amelia avoided travelling by train as much as possible, but it was the quickest way to get to the city from Coventry, so she had bitten the bullet and travelled to the station by train rather than car.

She had asked one of the station guards where the transport police were based and now sat in their cupboard of an office waiting for her DS and Dominic. At least she'd been offered a biscuit and a coffee. The coffee tasted bitter, so she was glad to have the sweet hobnob to dunk in it.

The transport cop grinned at her. "So, what's your interest? We don't get the NCA gracing us with their presence much." He had looked properly at her ID, then.

"County lines case. We deal with all sorts now."

The officer nodded. "Ah. Thought as much when Starley called. He deals with the young uns."

"Does he?"

"Oh yeah. He's sound, is Starley. They usually lead us a merry dance, but they don't bother with him." He winked. "Don't get them nowhere."

Amelia hadn't seen him as that authoritarian, but maybe he was different around kids.

"Did you find any footage of the girl?" Amelia thought she might as well get it lined up for the others as she didn't want to be stuck here longer than necessary.

The transport officer pressed a few buttons and the screens in front of her lit up. She spotted Aleesha Coleman immediately. She had her hand on the collar of a young kid's parka and was pulling him towards the toilets. A sullen young girl followed the pair. Catherine and Dominic arrived at that point to see Aleesha push the boy into the gents.

Catherine put her hand on the screen, recognising her errant niece. She took it away as soon as she realised the others were staring at her.

"Yep, that's the one. Thanks, John." Dominic patted the officer on the back.

Amelia hadn't even thought to ask his name. "Do you know which train they took?"

John grinned and pulled up another image. "The 12:40 to Plymouth. Oh, and before you ask, I've relayed a message to all the stations on the route, and they haven't disembarked yet."

"Whereabouts is the train now?" Amelia thought they might at least have an idea where they could be going.

John tapped away on a keyboard until he found the live times for the train. "It's currently at Bristol Parkway."

Amelia stared at the screen, trying to read all of the interim stations before Plymouth. She turned to Dominic. "Out of these, which do you think is the most likely?"

He shrugged. "It could be any of them for different reasons. Small towns or seaside towns are good markets. I'd be surprised if they went as far as Plymouth. They usually stick to areas a bit nearer... for example, in Warwickshire."

"She knows." Catherine wiped her forehead with her sleeve.

Amelia rubbed her colleague's arm in an attempt to soothe her pain. "Knows what?"

"That we're onto her."

She could well be right, but the more important question might be — who were the two kids that were with her?

"Can you go back to the original footage at New Street?"

John pulled that up on the larger screen.

"Catherine, do you recognise the other kids?" Amelia gestured at them.

Catherine shook her head.

"Do you?" Amelia turned to Dominic in the vain hope that he might recognise them as baby-faced gang members rather than the young children that they appeared to be.

"Not on our radar, I'm afraid."

"Is it just me that thinks they're about seven, maybe ten at the most?"

Dominic sighed. "It's not just you."

Whose kids were they? Surely someone was missing them.

Dominic must have read her mind. "I'll circulate their pictures to local stations and social services. A lot of these kids are known to them."

Catherine scowled. "I hope you're not suggesting —"

"Not all kids. Some come from nice, cosy middle-class homes. God knows why they'd decide that this shit's better."

Everyone stood in silence watching the live feed as the train made its journey towards the next station. It was now just outside Weston-Super-Mare, the destination of choice for many families in Coventry and Birmingham heading to the beach for a day trip. It would be ironic if this was where they left the train. Amelia's memories of the place were marred by the fact that she never really got to see the sea. Either it was too far out in the Bristol Channel, or her mum had forced her to play more daft games on the pier, so they'd missed its brief visit. Like most Midlanders, Amelia yearned for the sound of the sea — waves crashing onto the shore and the salty air. The water of the Birmingham canals did not have the same pull, unfortunately.

A few minutes later, the train pulled into Weston. The CCTV wasn't fantastic here but a grainy picture came up of a taller person and two youngsters who didn't seem very keen to be together.

"That's them." John seemed certain. Maybe he was used to the poor-quality images. This was his job with the Transport police, after all. He was already ringing through to the railway staff at the station.

Catherine jabbed at the screen with a finger and looked pointedly at Dominic. "Aren't you going to do anything?"

Dominic replied, calmly, "It's not my area of the country. I'll let the locals know."

To be fair, he already had his phone in his hand.

Amelia understood Catherine's concern. This was her niece. But there was no way anyone could intercept them from here. You couldn't chase a train in a car. This wasn't the movies. The local force would have handled many cases like this before. They might already know which B&Bs to search for wayward kids.

Catherine hadn't finished. "This is *your* fault," she accused Dominic. "You knew my niece was at risk, yet you've done nothing to protect her!"

She was waving her arms around now and everyone took a step back except Amelia. She moved towards her colleague with her hands open in front of her.

"It's okay, Cath." She pulled her colleague towards her in a hug and held her while she sobbed.

Amelia would have reacted in the same way if it was one of her kids. She didn't blame Catherine at all.

But Catherine was having none of it. A few seconds later, she pushed Amelia away and marched towards the door. "I'll sort it myself, then!"

There was no point in following her. She'd likely soon run out of steam and, no doubt, end up at her sister's. Amelia would ring her later to offer support, maybe even speak to Pat to see if they could release Catherine on family leave for a couple of days if she needed it.

Dominic turned to Amelia, then said what she had been thinking for the past hour: "Aleesha's in this big time. That —" he pointed back to the screen, "— is child abduction."

Chapter 9

Contact

Catherine didn't turn up for work that evening and wasn't answering Amelia's calls. Sean offered to stay the night, but that wouldn't have been fair. He'd done his shift. This was his downtime. Amelia knew she'd have to report this to Pat but didn't relish the idea. She'd give her this evening then that would be it. It wasn't like Amelia had never gone AWOL or been a lone ranger. She could work one night without her sergeant and call Sean if there were any problems.

She spent the first couple of hours checking the factory every few minutes and logging what she spotted. A few visitors came and went. They weren't here to fish the canals or to take out packages of goods. They were here purely to pay for sex. Brazenly, they took the metal steps two at a time, full of immoral purpose.

Amelia didn't care that they paid for sex, but these were not women who had a choice. If the men wanted sex, she could point them in the direction of internet sites that could hook them up with escorts working safely from Birmingham homes. But they were more expensive and forced them to behave in a particular way. It was never completely safe.

As she worked, she had the radio on in the background. She never bothered with music but liked to listen to well-spoken actors in radio plays, finding it quite soothing even if she couldn't hear the words.

It must have moved on to the news. *Pandemic... China... lockdown... rise... death.*

A man in jeans ran down the staircase, nearly slipping on the metal stairs. Amelia grabbed her jacket and bag, hoping the flashlight was still in the pocket.

Getting off a boat was just as difficult as getting on. She chose to exit via the well deck as it meant that she wouldn't have to climb the steps to go out the stern doors. Pushing open the wooden doors, she almost slipped on the wet boards but just managed to right herself and step over the side onto the towpath. She left the doors swinging. She didn't care if anyone peered in. They wouldn't see much anyway as the boat was in darkness.

She jogged down the towpath hoping that she couldn't be heard, wanting to see where this man was going in such a hurry but not wanting to draw attention to herself in the meantime. Fortunately, the towpath was clear of obstacles and her stride was much longer than his; she reached the bridge just as he crossed it in her direction. Just in time, she was able to duck back behind a brick wall. She held her breath. He was slowing now, panting hard. This gave her the opportunity to peer around the edge of the wall. He'd stopped and was bent double, holding his thighs. She could make out his features, more European than Asian. A punter? Probably.

Now it seemed more important to get back to the factory to try to discover what had led to his flight. Amelia walked back to the boat, hands in her pockets, just another midnight walker returning home from the pub. When she reached the bow of her narrowboat, she stepped back in, closed the doors and returned to the laptop screens. She checked each of the hidden cameras in turn, cursing under her breath that she was alone. A partner would have been handy right now.

Nothing seemed untoward. It took a while before the camera on the lower floor picked up a young woman crying. Amelia zoomed in as much as she could and noticed the woman holding the top of her nose. A darker smudge of colour surrounded her mouth and chin, dripping to the floor. The bastard had hit her in the face. That's all that Amelia could assume by her actions. Another reason to end this operation.

The rest of the night passed without incident. Amelia kept checking her phone to see if Catherine had got in touch. She decided to ring her first thing in the morning and, if she didn't answer, she'd go and see Pat. There was only so much covering she could do. She just hoped that her sergeant hadn't gone to Weston-Super-Mare on a wild goose chase.

At first light, Amelia yawned and went in search of coffee. The coffee jar was practically empty and there was only enough milk left for one cup. She could text one of the lads to pick some up on the way, but she needed to stretch her legs. There was a local shop about half a mile away that she thought would be open early. Customers were always going in and out, whatever hour she left for "work" in the morning. After finding her bag and jacket, Amelia left the boat and stumbled out into the early morning mist. The air stung her face. It seemed much colder this morning than it had on her late-night run.

She crossed the bridge as the shop was nearer to the factory than the boat. Amelia hadn't gone far when she overheard voices.

"Don't be long. You've got a list and I'm

timing you," a man growled.

"Okay," a much softer voice responded.

Then Amelia heard the familiar sound of footsteps on the metal staircase. She hung back a little to make sure they reached the towpath ahead of her. If she was lucky, this young woman was heading for the shop, too.

A few minutes later, the woman swung off the towpath and up the path beside the next bridge to the road ahead.

Amelia followed her, quickening her pace slightly. As she drew nearer to the woman, she called, "Hey, slow down. I can't keep up with you."

The woman turned, her mouth forming an O shape. Then her lips quickly clamped back together. She did not speak and kept walking.

Amelia didn't give up. She reached the woman and nudged her arm.

"I'm Amy. I live on the boat just down there." She pointed back toward the canal. "I'm just getting milk. Trust us to run out… and I've got work in less than an hour."

The woman still ignored her. Now Amelia was close, she could see the bruise on the bridge of her nose. It was spreading to the edge of her eyelid. This was the woman that had been beaten last night, most likely.

Amelia grabbed her arm this time. "Hey, are you okay? You look hurt."

The woman stopped now and glanced around her, shuffling her feet as though she was looking for an escape route.

Amelia continued, "If you need help then I'm sure I can do something. You only have to say. If everything's fine, then don't say a word and we'll just walk to the shop together. I can take a hint." She slipped her arm through the younger girl's arm and strode on.

The woman could only comply.

As they neared the shop, the woman muttered, "I'm okay. Honest."

Amelia whispered, "You don't look it. If someone's hurting you —"

"They're not. I fell over. I'm just staying there with my husband until we find somewhere to live. You won't tell anyone?"

"Course not." Amelia pretended to zip her lips. "Your secret's safe with me. What's your name?"

"Julie... my name's Julie."

"Julie?"

"Yes, my mother liked musicals."

Amelia tried not to laugh. But she'd call her Julie if that's what she wanted to be called. At least she was speaking now. "Can't be easy living in an empty factory. I mean, the boat's bad enough — but a big, empty space? Must be freezing."

The woman smiled. "We have blankets and each other."

Amelia didn't want to betray that she knew that she was lying. "How sweet. I guess you don't have to be as close as I do to my smelly boyfriend. He works nights and I work days, so we don't even get the chance to snuggle up. It sucks."

They'd reached the shop, so Amelia dropped her arm. "Why don't we get our shopping and meet outside then can walk back together?"

"No," Julie snapped, then softened. "I've got a list of things to get and I don't want to keep you... you've got work."

Amelia sighed. "You're right. I've got work. But I'm sure we'll see each other again, eh?"

It didn't take Amelia long to get coffee,

milk and a couple of packets of biscuits. She looked for Julie but couldn't see her as she left. It was a start, a way in that she'd share with the lads when she got back to the boat.

Pat didn't look pleased. She tapped the desk and scowled. "For God's sake, Amelia! You should have told me last night. And she's not even answering her phone?"

"No." She'd tried a couple of times and nothing.

"Bollocks! Have you got time to drive to her place before you knock off?"

"Sure." Her kids would be at school now and Callum had Baby Sensory on a Tuesday so she wouldn't even see him before hitting the sack. What was sleep, anyway?

Pat relaxed back in her chair. "We might have a problem… with this bloody virus thing."

What bloody virus?

She must have looked vacant as Pat continued. "You know – the one from Wuhan. It's been on all the news… and don't tell me you haven't been reading your emails, hen."

Amelia had, of course, heard about the virus and knew there had been some cases in the UK. "It's only going to be like swine flu, surely? A storm in a teacup."

"It may well be, but I've been told to review all our cases and define what's essential as we may be needed elsewhere."

"Are they predicting food riots or summat?"

"They're predicting deaths... lots of them."

Seriously?

"I'll know more tomorrow. We've got a briefing from the big boss herself."

"Must be important, then. You're off to London for the day, then?"

"You're kidding, right? It's all online. Have to sign into it. You don't think they'll pay to accommodate any of us, do you? Anyway, keep washing your hands. And, Amelia, let me know if you catch up with Catherine. If we've sorted her some leave or she's back at work tonight, then I'll turn a blind eye. Any longer though —"

Amelia stood up to go. "Yeah, sure."

As she left Pat's office, she almost crashed into Jason Starling. He muttered, "Sorry."

"No worries. Are you after Pat?' Amelia always wondered what the use of civilians in the service was, particularly this one.

"Actually, I wanted to speak to you." He took the top of his pen with his teeth. "I need to update your settings for the shared drives. Can I borrow your laptop or just have your password?"

"I'm busy right now. It'll have to be later." Amelia didn't have time for this, and there was no way she'd just hand over her password.

"I wouldn't normally ask but Pat's on my tail to get everything sorted quickly. We've got to be set up for remote working."

"When I get back…" Amelia didn't wait for a response and headed back to her desk to fetch her bag.

Catherine didn't answer the door at home, and Amelia didn't know her sister's address but guessed it would be the same as Aleesha's. She rang Dominic. He didn't answer, so she left him a voicemail asking him to send her the address as soon as he could.

She might as well head home. If Catherine's sister lived somewhere in Coventry, she'd be better off at home anyway.

Halfway down the motorway, a text message pinged. Her dash showed that it was from Dominic and that he'd provided an address. Amelia knew the street. It was a cul-de-sac in the Stoke area of the city, on the border of Hillfields, not too far from the city centre and RB7 territory.

Fifty minutes later, Amelia was knocking on the white UPVC door of Catherine's sister's house. A small woman still in her dressing gown and slippers opened the door. Amelia smiled at her. "Hi, Marsha. It's Amelia, Catherine's partner. Can I come in?"

Before Marsha could even consider closing the door, Amelia was inside. She glanced at the various doors in the hall. "Is Catherine here?"

Marsha shuffled towards the door at the far end. "No, she's not. I can make you a cuppa, though."

Amelia was surprised at her hospitality. "Great. Thank you."

Marsha nodded towards the other door. "Go in and take a seat. I won't be long. Tea or coffee?"

Amelia headed for what she assumed would be the lounge. "Coffee, milk, no sugar. Thanks."

The lounge was a knock-through with an electric fire and brick surround. A huge corner sofa dominated the room. Amelia cleared away some papers and sat down. A number of mugs cluttered the coffee table but, by the state of them, Amelia didn't reckon that she'd had guests. It was more likely that she'd nested here since her daughter had left. The family photos on the wall showed only Aleesha and Catherine, her husband and kids. Amelia guessed that Aleesha had no siblings or none that Marsha was proud of.

Marsha brought her a coffee and a drink for herself. She sat at the other end of the sofa and muttered, "Sorry about the mess."

She looked so much older than Catherine and could easily be mistaken for her aunt or mother, not her sister. Her weave was much tighter and greying at the roots. Her face was a study of lines and acne scars.

"Have you had any word on Aleesha, Mrs Coleman"

"No. Nothing. I've had the social round, but they're not interested. She's over sixteen now." She reached for her vape and took a long draw. As she did so, her sleeve fell back revealing scars in the crook of her arm. A drug user, maybe? They looked healed, so maybe she was clean now, but it would explain why she'd aged so badly.

"Have you seen Catherine? She hasn't been at work." There was no point in small talk.

Marsha coughed and reached for a tissue from the box on the table. She wiped her mouth before she spoke. "She won't come here."

"Why not?"

Marsha waved her arm around the room. "She might dirty her suit."

Chalk and cheese. Amelia once imagined having a sister until she realised that having a sister meant another child putting up with her mother's abuse. But she knew that sisters didn't always see eye to eye, and many didn't even speak.

"Have you spoken to Catherine? I'm worried about her."

"She's rung me, yeah. To have a go." She

sucked on her vape. "She seems to think she can do a better job with Aleesha. Just wait until her young 'uns turn into teenagers. You got kids?"

"Yeah, three." Amelia smiled. "One's a teenager, the other's still in Primary and I've got one in nappies. I do need to get home and see them, actually."

"Don't let me stop you."

Amelia wondered if it was worth appealing to her but decided not to bother. She stood and gave Marsha her card. "If Catherine gets in touch, tell her to ring me urgently — and let me know that you've spoken to her, would you?"

Marsha took the card and placed it on top of one of the mugs. "Bye then. Don't worry about the mug. I'll get round to washing it eventually."

Becky was sitting at the kitchen table doing her homework when Amelia arrived home. She leaned back in her chair and rubbed at her fingers. "Christ, my hands are sore!"

"Working hard?" Amelia picked up the kettle. "Tea?"

"Thanks. A green one." She picked her pen back up. "It's not work. It's all this handwashing we have to do. It's driving us all mad."

"Handwashing? Don't blame them having a hygiene drive with you bunch of smelly teenagers."

"It's so we don't spread germs with this virus thingy." Becky stared at her mum. "Should we be worried?"

"How would I know? It's probably all a flash in the pan."

Her mum, Jane, came into the kitchen

followed by her tottering son.

"Wow, look at you! Your walking's really coming along!"

Her mum harrumphed as if to say that she'd know that if she was ever home. "Can you talk to Caitlyn? She seems to think we can take her to boxing three times a week and I've not got the time to take her."

"Sure," Amelia sighed.

Caitlyn was in her bedroom building a Lego tower. She seemed to spend more time in there since Callum had become more mobile. It was probably a good thing, as no one wanted to take him to A and E with a plastic brick shoved up his nose.

"What's this about boxing?"

"Michal says if I want to progress, I need to train harder."

"Did he now?" He could have asked her first — but that would mean he'd have to speak to her.

"There's a class three times a week after school, so I thought I could go to all of them."

"That's lovely, Caitlyn. But how would you get there and back, and when would you do your homework?"

"I'm only in Year 5. I don't get that much."

At the last parents' evening, which Jola had attended on Amelia's behalf, her teacher had said that Caitlyn excelled at Maths and Science but was falling behind with her reading and writing. They had an agreement that she'd read at least one chapter of a book each week. Amelia glanced around the bedroom. No books in sight. She could broach the subject or leave it.

Her daughter scowled. "Ask Michal to pick

me up. I'm sure he would if you asked him."

Would he? Surely this wasn't something he'd cooked up with Caitlyn to see more of her.

"Okay. I'll speak to Michal, but you still need to study. Where's the book you're reading this week?"

Her daughter stood, went over to her bed and lifted the pillow. "This one?" It was one of the Harry Potter books, which explained the Lego tower that looked like Hogwarts by the look of the box.

"Who got you this?"

Caitlyn added another brick. "You did, Mum, for my birthday last month."

Amelia stood and before she left muttered, "Just testing."

Jane sat knitting in the living room with her feet up. "Did you get any sleep today?"

Amelia looked at her watch. *Shit.* She had to leave in ten minutes or she'd be late for her shift. "I've got to go. I'll take something out of the freezer and heat it up on the boat later. I'll ring Michal, too, and sort this thing with Caitlyn."

Her phone flashed up Catherine's name as soon as she started her car.

A text appeared: I'M IN TROUBLE, SORRY.

Chapter 10

Catherine

Instead of driving to the boat, Amelia texted the lads to tell them they'd need to stay on for an extra hour or so. She couldn't help thinking back to the last time she'd received such a message.

I'M IN TROUBLE. On that occasion, it had been Jake, and that had cost the life of her former partner, Chloe. Hopefully, this time she could help her colleague without any blood being shed.

Amelia picked up her phone and rang Catherine. She answered almost immediately.

"I'm sorry."

Amelia could barely hear her above the background noise. It sounded like she was in the midst of traffic.

"Where are you?"

"On the M6. I'm heading back to Brum. I couldn't find Aleesha. I had to look. Sorry."

Amelia let out a breath of relief. "It's fine. I'd have done the same."

"I know. But I should've called you, at least. I wasn't sure if you'd let me go."

"It wouldn't be down to me."

"I know. I guess you've told Pat that I went AWOL."

"I had to. I didn't know if you were safe." Amelia paused. "But it's fine. Get to the boat some time tonight and Pat will turn a blind eye.'

"Thanks. I need to see my family first. Are you okay on your own for a bit?"

She'd have to be. "Sure."

Catherine rang off.

Of course, Amelia would have done the

same, but she'd have told her boss what she was doing. No, actually, she wouldn't. Who was she trying to kid? She'd have behaved in exactly the same way.

Catherine didn't get to the boat until after midnight. By that time, Amelia had completed a load of outstanding paperwork as well as keeping a watchful eye on the factory. Everything had been quiet on that front with hardly any visitors at all. Those that had entered the building left half an hour later, sated.

Her colleague looked exhausted.

"Coffee?" It always took ages to boil the kettle on the Calor gas stove. By the time it whistled, Amelia hoped to have learned as much as she could about Catherine's efforts to find Aleesha.

Catherine rubbed her eyes. "Thanks. Hopefully, it'll keep me awake."

That reminded Amelia that she hadn't managed many hours of sleep herself over the last few days, either. She sat down opposite her partner at the dinette. "How did you get on?"

"I didn't find her. Not a whisper of her."

"Did you expect to?"

"Not really." She folded her arms tight as though trying to hold herself together. "Hoped, maybe. The station guards at Weston didn't see them leave the train. The CCTV showed them heading towards the seafront but it's not like a city with every corner covered. The local police were kind but didn't hold out much hope of finding them. There are so many places they could go — B&Bs, private flats, squats, you name it."

"But you went to the locals for help?"

"Yeah. Seemed the most sensible thing to do."

Amelia had images of her partner stopping people on the street with a photo of her niece. But, of course, she'd have sought help from the local force first once she'd calmed down.

"I met your sister, by the way."

It was clear by Catherine's reaction that she hadn't wanted that.

"She's not the best mum in the world but she doesn't deserve to lose her daughter."

"My mum was the same... well, she was an alcoholic. I pretty much went off the rails, too."

"What brought you back?"

Amelia bit her lip. "I got pregnant and tried to self-abort."

"Oh!"

"My mum found me in the bath, fortunately, or I might not be here."

"I'm glad." Catherine smiled. "That she found you, I mean."

Amelia filled her partner in about speaking to the woman from the warehouse. It was a start. Maybe they'd see her again and build on her trust. Or maybe they wouldn't.

The rest of the night passed without incident. They took it in turns to have a nap while the other worked. They were both able to go home at a reasonable time too, which was a bonus.

Amelia awoke with a start and realised that she hadn't put her work phone on silent mode. The ping was a text from Pat: CHECK YOUR EMAILS.

She sat up in bed, placing a couple of

pillows behind her back and did just that. Approximately fifty emails had come in whilst she'd slept. The usual crap. The vast majority wouldn't need to be followed up. The one that Pat was referring to was marked with a red exclamation mark and the subject line was in red text. *For immediate action: please read for your new assignments.*

This was all she needed. With some trepidation, she opened the email, hoping that she wouldn't be moving to online surveillance. She wasn't. But two of those working on the operation were: Catherine and Amir were to move to CEOP by the end of the week. Amelia was to continue to work on her usual cases but with a number of caveats. She'd need a coffee before she even attempted to read these.

Amelia entered the kitchen to find her mother taking something out of the oven.

"I made too much fish pie. Do you want some?"

"For breakfast?" Amelia reached for a mug and was pleased to see that the cafetière was full of freshly brewed coffee.

"I'll put some aside for you later."

"Are the kids back yet?"

"Caitlyn's walked to boxing from school. Michal's giving her some one-to-one since she can't make the sessions."

Amelia wished they'd run this past her first. "When was this decided?"

"She said you knew." *But I haven't agreed to it.* "And the school's okay with her walking there on her own. They're letting Years 5 and 6 walk home on their own as part of a trial this term. You had a letter to sign."

She didn't recall signing anything, but it wouldn't be the first time that her kids had thrust something into her hands at the last minute that she'd barely read. But it was Michal that she was more cross with. Why did he think it was okay to undermine her? She grabbed her bag and car keys.

"Where are you going?" Her mother shouted after her. "At least finish your coffee."

It took half an hour to reach the gym, far longer than normal. Traffic seemed to move at a snail's pace, which only added to Amelia's cross mood. She'd realised as soon as she got in the car that this wasn't a sensible thing to do. It was clear from Pat's email that business as usual would be short-lived. The kids might not be even going to school in a few weeks. Why else would they be changing their assignments so quickly? But perhaps, more importantly, did she want a showdown with Michal? That could well be the end of them. The ties that bound them together were the finest of threads.

Michal was standing proud in the centre of the ring when Amelia arrived, giving one-to-one tuition to a svelte young boxer. He didn't spot her at first. When he did, he touched the boxer on the shoulder. "Shall we take five? Go and hydrate."

He then left the ring, holding up the top rope and stepping through with ease.

"Sorry to interrupt your session," Amelia muttered.

Michal pulled her into an unexpected hug. Amelia wasn't as fleet of foot as Michal's proteges and couldn't move fast enough to avoid it. Instead, she found herself sinking in closer.

When she eventually pulled away, she felt flushed and anxious. "Shall we talk in the office?"

"Sure." Michal walked ahead, seemingly unaware of her inner turmoil.

As soon as the office door shut, Amelia sighed. "You need to run things past me."

Michal scowled, "Like what?"

"You know what. Letting Caitlyn come here after school. She's only just turned ten."

"And she's got a ton of potential." Michal stopped short of slamming the desk. "This is what she wants to do — or have you not bothered to ask her?"

Amelia sat back in her chair realising that it was this passion that had attracted her in the first place. Why was she so angry now?

Michal must have sensed her pause. "If it's the walk here that bothers you, I can pick her up."

It wasn't that. "What are we doing, Michal?"

"Doing?" He shrugged. "Discussing your daughter and her boxing."

"No... us, I mean."

Michal sighed and leaned forward. "I don't know, Amelia. You tell me."

"It's you..." Amelia studied him, hoping for some clue of what he desired to happen in the future.

Silence filled the gap, highlighting the gulf between them.

Eventually, Michal spoke. "I killed a man. You might be used to it —"

"I've never killed anyone." And she hadn't. There weren't many police officers who had.

"Then you don't know how I feel."

"Tell me."

"I look at you, Amelia, and I see that bastard lying there in your bedroom. And I killed him."

"So you don't want to see me at all?"

Michal reached out and took Amelia's hand in his. "Of course I do."

What did she want? Now was the time to say.

"Maybe if we saw more of each other, you'd start just thinking of me and not him."

Is that what she wanted? She'd said it now. She'd put her heart on the line.

Michal smiled. "Yeah, you could well be right. How about dinner on Saturday?"

So did this mean that he wanted to see more of her?

Amelia didn't know if she'd be working. There wasn't much point in watching the factory all the time, particularly since her staff would be reduced after Monday and they'd have to cut back. "Yeah, I'd like that."

They parted with a hug, leaving Amelia just enough time to drive to WMROC to see Pat. The rules listed in her email that morning were burning through her skull. How dare anyone even suggest that she didn't know how to wash her hands! Social distancing was her usual go-to, unless, of course, the other person was Michal, who never gave her any choice about getting up close and personal. He was the only person who'd ever got away with hugging her.

Pat was packing her bag ready to leave for the day when Amelia entered her office. She didn't look up. "This better be quick, Amelia. I've got yet another meeting with Head Office."

"That email. You've gotta be kidding me. I'm not losing my team."

Pat sat down, no doubt realising that Amelia meant business. "You know what's going on, right?"

"What do you mean?"

Pat picked up a pencil and started tapping it on her desk. "We're in the middle of a global pandemic, in case you haven't noticed. You're not the only one affected by this."

"Are you trying to say I'm selfish?" Amelia demanded like a petulant teenager. "It's more about the women locked in that factory than me."

"I know it's hard, but it's not like they're going anywhere."

"Well, surely that's the point. Have they received a stupid email telling them about face coverings and two-metre rules??

"Listen, Amelia. There's talk of a lockdown. Within weeks, shops like the nail bar will be shut. We may even get food shortages, riots —"

"That's just conjecture. It's not like we've had many cases —"

"But we're expecting them and we have to plan." Pat stopped tapping and stared at Amelia. "We need Catherine at CEOP. If the schools shut, loads of kids are going to be online and vulnerable. Not every family's lucky enough to have a nanny to keep an eye on their kids, so we have to."

"For fuck's sake! Don't bring my family into this to score points." Amelia stood up. Pat shrank back a little in her chair. "I get it. But the women in the factory are vulnerable, too, and who'll be there to keep an eye on them?"

"You will. I haven't taken you off the case. Obviously, you and Sean will need some sort of rota and I can't give you any overtime, so stick to it."

"No overtime?"

"None. We're going to need the staff and money for more important things like possibly quelling unrest."

Jola had mentioned something about there being very little toilet paper left at the supermarket that week. Were they facing food fights in the aisles?

"This is bollocks and you know it. When we had swine flu, there were like twenty cases in the whole division and no one was that ill. It's just going to be like that. It'll all be over in a week."

"No, Amelia, it won't," Pat sighed. "You can have Catherine for another two weeks. That's the best I can do. Now, if you don't mind, I need to leave."

Amelia stood.

"Your PPE pack's on your desk, by the way. Don't go without it."

Amelia expected it to be branded NCA like pretty much everything these days and was surprised to find it that contained packs of plain black face masks, disposable gloves and a bottle of hand sanitiser along with another How To Wash Your Hands leaflet. She stuffed them in her backpack.

Will, who was in charge of intelligence on the case, motioned her over to his desk. He waited until she perched on the edge of the seat opposite. "I've got something for you."

"Great. Fire away."

"Those photos you sent us on Tuesday — we've got a match." Will turned the laptop around so she could see. He pointed to a photo of a South Asian male speaking into a mobile. "This guy, Lee Cheun, he's wanted on a bail breach."

"What's the offence?"

84

"Aggravated assault, GBH. He attacked a restaurant owner in Chinatown last year. It still hasn't gone to court, but he's missed a couple of check-ins at his local police station."

"Looks like he's still around, then. Part of a gang?"

Will nodded. "Possibly Triad but we've got nothing recorded. No tattoos listed on his arrest record."

"That doesn't mean anything." Amelia pointed at the photo. "Any associates? Do we have any idea where he could be in the pecking order?"

"Not that high up, I imagine."

That was likely to be true. The higher up you were, the less likely it was that you'd be caught with a weapon. This guy was cannon fodder but he might give Amelia more leverage for keeping staff on her team. This was their first named suspect, at least.

"Send me his file. Thanks, Will. Good work."

Chapter 11

First Deaths

Becky was sitting at the dining room table writing up a science experiment with the radio tuned to a local station. Amelia sat opposite her cradling a coffee, not wanting to disturb her elder daughter but enjoying her company nonetheless.

When had she grown so tall? It almost felt as though she had missed stretches of time when her daughter had left childhood and progressed to womanhood, time that wouldn't be recovered. How had she missed that? A faint smile graced her lips as she raised the patterned mug for another long gulp.

"You going to sit there watching me, Mum?" Becky raised her eyebrows as she spoke, reminding Amelia for the third time that week how much she looked like her dead father.

"Sorry. I didn't mean to stare. Shall I leave you be?"

Becky shrugged. "No. S'okay."

"What work are you doing?"

Becky put her pen down and shut her laptop. "None, now."

"I'll —"

"Haven't you got a case file to be looking at in your office?"

"I just thought…" Amelia made a move to get up.

Becky grinned. "It's okay, Mum. I'm kidding. I'm supposed to be writing up a chemistry practical, but to be honest, I'm not really into it and it doesn't need to be in until Monday."

The news headlines began. *This morning, Birmingham had its first death from*

Coronavirus.

Amelia shuddered. "Turn it off. It's all I've heard all day."

Becky paled. "But… Mum, it's serious, isn't it?"

"Is it?"

"It's all they're talking about at school. We have to wash our hands about twenty times a day and one of the teachers even suggested we sing nursery rhymes. I'm bloody fifteen, Mum, not four."

Amelia giggled at this and Becky joined in.

"At least you haven't been given silly facemasks to wear. Hang on." Amelia retrieved her backpack from the hall. She lifted out her laptop and placed it on the table, followed by her pack of PPE goodies. "This is what I got from work today."

"At least yours are black." Becky held up a facemask. "Those blue disposable medical ones are so bleurgh."

At just that moment, Caitlyn bounded into the dining room. "Try it on, Mum."

"Fit!" Becky giggled.

Amelia put the facemask on. It felt tight, so she adjusted her hair, which was caught up in it.

Caitlyn grabbed her phone out of her back pocket. "Let me take a pic."

"No chance." Amelia pulled off the mask. "We'll all be wearing them soon enough, then I can laugh at you two."

A few hours later, the usual level of Barton family seriousness returned when Amelia sat on her own in her office, poring over the file Will had sent her. She'd decided she'd be better served doing some work at home before heading for the boat. Still annoyed that they'd be expected to drop everything at any point, she wanted to concentrate on the offender.

Lee Cheun had arrived in the UK in 2003. His home address was a flat above a Chinese takeaway in Bordesley Green. The offence he was running from was the only one recorded but may or may not be the only one committed. He had leave to remain under the Hong Kong agreement. There were no known associates or gang ties listed, which didn't mean much since he had no other convictions. He may have just been lucky not to be caught.

He was one of the foot soldiers paid to keep the women and men in the warehouse in line, like the supervisor at the nail bar, just one step above the slaves and making very little money from it. Above them were the real gangmasters.

That's why she was carrying out surveillance at the factory. They needed more intelligence, or else what was the point? They might as well just enter the factory tonight, release the captives and arrest Lee Cheun. But then, of course, they'd be faced with an impenetrable wall of silence and any hope of finding those above them would be lost. They always had to think of the long-term gain. The women were such a small part of the picture, and some would say they were insignificant. That's what always angered Amelia.

A ping announced an email from Pat. Amelia opened it, expecting a rota for the three of them to cover the next week. Instead, it was short and blunt. *First death in Birmingham recorded with another three people in intensive care. Expect to move to new assignments by the end of the week if not sooner.*

Nothing about Catherine, so maybe she could keep her, at least in the short term.

By midnight, Amelia couldn't keep her eyes on the screen any longer. She shut the laptop and decided that she'd be better off joining Catherine on the boat. At least she could find out how her partner felt about the whole situation and would be better placed to judge the best way to protect this current crop of and future crops of captives, both in the short and long term.

Catherine was eating a lasagne ready meal when Amelia got to the boat. She paused. "Do you want some?"

Amelia realised how hungry she was. "Only if there's some going spare."

Fortunately, Catherine had only eaten half of the pasta. The other half was left in the tray, and she dished it up on a plate and handed it to her boss. "I was going to save it until later if I got peckish. Night shifts play havoc with my appetite."

"Mine, too." But then Amelia didn't have to cope with the extra complication of diabetes as her partner did.

"I was thinking." Catherine pushed her plate away, having finished her meal. "I might quite enjoy working at CEOP. At least I might get a handle on Aleesha. Who knows where she could be right now?"

Maybe no one had told Catherine that Amelia had managed to hang on to her for an extra two weeks? Perhaps Amelia wasn't being fair. She hadn't even thought of Catherine's wishes. "Pat says you can stay on this case for an extra two weeks. If you want to, that is."

"Oh." There was a pause. "I see. Well,

I'm happy to if you need me, but to be honest, there's not much happening."

This was true. What had they achieved? They'd discovered that Lee Cheun was minding the women, and Amelia had spoken to one of them. They'd made copious notes about visitors, clarifying that the place was being run as a brothel. But that was it.

"I'll call Pat in the morning. CEOP needs you more."

An hour later, Amelia could feel herself dropping off. She sat up straight in the hope that she'd feel more awake. She felt, at the same time as she heard it, the boat rock angrily against the side of the bank. Then she heard a shout. She shot to her feet, banging her head against the ceiling, forgetting that the sides of the boat had less headroom than the middle. Catherine must have heard it, too, and had already moved to the front of the boat. She grappled with the lock until it came loose then flung the doors open, looking very much the archetypal pissed-off boater.

"Hey! What the fuck are you doing at this time of night?"

If the two men thought it was odd that she was dressed in jeans and a T-shirt at 3 o'clock in the morning, they didn't show it. Amelia stood behind Catherine, just out of sight.

"None of your fucking business," one of the men spluttered.

The other guy seemed to want to use the distraction as an opportunity to escape but, unfortunately, he was spotted. The more aggressive of the two men, who Amelia now saw was Cheun, grabbed the other guy by the scruff of his neck and then pulled him closer. In an act of pure pretence, he threw his arm further around his shoulder like they were best buddies who'd just had a drunken spat.

"Sorry. Must have forgotten ourselves for a minute and didn't mean to disturb you. Did we, Andy?"

Andy, if that was his name, didn't protest or even try to move. Maybe he was resigned to his fate. Amelia decided to make herself known.

Cheun grinned. "Sorry. Didn't realise you were a couple of lezzers."

Catherine stepped back and threw her arm around Amelia. "That's right. I didn't realise you two were gay, either."

Cheun moved away from the other bloke who took this as his cue to scarper. "Don't be so fucking ridiculous."

"Yeah, you're right. What bloke in their right mind — or woman for that matter — would fancy you?" Catherine continued to jibe.

He must have realised that there was no point taking this pair of women on. They weren't worth his time and, besides, he'd now lost his prey. He sulked off without looking back.

Catherine turned to Amelia. "Is that him, then?"

So she's read Will's file. Amelia nodded.

"Doesn't look up to much, does he?"

"No," Amelia agreed. "What do you reckon? The other guy's a punter?"

"Or a gambler."

"Gambler?"

"Yeah. I spotted the other day they've got a back room that seems to get quite busy. Only blokes going in and out. Could be drugs or gambling."

Amelia hadn't considered gambling. She didn't know much about the illegal side. They

91

needed an expert. Gambling, drugs and prostitution led by a Chinese OCG? The women seemed to be mostly Southeast Asian. She fired off an email to Will asking him to arrange a link up with a Chinese organised crime expert.

Chapter 12

Thawing

The Undertaker opened the chest freezer with a gloved hand. A thin layer of ice shrouded the length of the plastic-covered package. First, he touched the head, gently brushing away the residue that had built up over the last couple of years. Then he gently lifted the whole body out of its frozen grave.

It was time to place her where she could finally be found.

Chapter 13
Chloe

Amelia woke early, driven by the urge to see her kids before they went to school. Maybe if she could get off the M6 quickly enough, she could even have breakfast with them. The ominous feeling that much was going to change in a short time dug away in her mind, clawing its way to the present.

Half an hour later, it seemed that all the other drivers must have had the same idea as her car crawled to a halt behind an impatient line of traffic.

Amelia slammed her hands on the steering wheel. "For fuck's sake!"

At precisely that moment, her phone chirped. She leant over and pushed the link button on her dashboard to answer. "Yeah?"

"Amelia. It's Pat." The line crackled. "Yeah?"

"We've found a body." There was a pause. "We think it's her."

Her. There was only one "her".

"Who?" Amelia barely whispered, needing to be sure. Eyes focussed ahead, she had to move in case it was her.

A whispered reply: "Chloe."

Tears, quick and sudden, flowed, leaving Amelia unable to speak.

"I'll send you the coordinates." Immediately, Amelia could see the flashing dot appear on her satnav. Six miles — thirty minutes away in this traffic.

She flipped open the box behind the handbrake and took out the portable blue light for use in an emergency situation. Her fingers stumbled over opening the window. When it was fully open, Amelia placed the bulb on top of

her car. The flashing light had little effect
to begin with. She could almost hear the sighs
as the cars in front of her began to move.
Slowly, they made a passable space, and she
was able to pull out onto the white lines
between the middle and fast lanes. The time it
would take to reach Chloe began to fall as she
sped up.

It wasn't long before she reached the
next motorway junction and only then did she
realise that she'd been biting her lip so hard
that it had bled. Pink tears dribbled down her
chin. She wiped them away with her jacket
sleeve. Fortunately, the dark grey material
hid a multitude of sins — usually coffee
stains and crumbs, not anything so primal.

Deep breaths helped, as did breaking the
speed limit through the urban streets leading
back into the centre of Brum. Nine minutes
away. Her foot hovered on the brake as she
spotted women with pushchairs and lines of
children on the pavements, the matching royal
blue jumpers catching her eye just in time.
The walk to school had started and she needed
to be more vigilant. She slowed. Ten minutes
away.

Finally, she reached the empty factories
along the canal. One minute away. Would Chloe
have been placed like the others, on show to
anyone venturing this way to work? Maybe an
early labourer or dog walker had discovered
her? What state would she find her in? They'd
better have covered her up and kept her safe.
Chloe was one of their own.

The white tent had already been erected.
Amelia exhaled. Before exiting the car, she
wiped her face with the towel she kept in the
glove compartment. Now all she needed to do
was put on her white suit and take control of

her shaking hands before her colleagues saw
her.

It was too late. Catherine had arrived
first. "You okay, boss?"

No, she wasn't okay. "Of course."

Pulling on the jumpsuit, she nearly
toppled over. Her long, gangly legs had never
been graceful, but she felt even more like a
newborn foal today.

Catherine touched her arm. "You don't
have to do this."

Amelia scowled at her. "Of course I
fucking do!"

Catherine stepped back, giving Amelia
space to pull on the shoe covers and walk
freely to the tent.

Without hesitation, she raised the side
flap. Chloe sat in front of her. She'd been
placed on a high mound of mud for all to see.
She knew it was Chloe despite the blast damage
to one side of her head and face. Bizarrely,
she still had some of her blond hair, which
stood to spiky attention. One of her ears
still held the five silver studs that Chloe
had always worn.

It almost looked like she was slouching
on a settee watching television. Her hands had
been placed in her lap, palms up. Her legs
were straight out in front of her. Her clothes
looked stale, grubby and crumpled, but were
intact. There was no sign of her T-shirt or
chinos having been removed. Even the laces on
her trainers were tied. Remarkably, she looked
as well-preserved as if she'd died only hours
ago.

"She's spent some time in a freezer," the
pathologist stated as though reading her mind.
"There are some freezer burn marks and
slippage, but that's why she's mostly intact.

I wouldn't bet on it, but she may have been buried for a short period, too."

"And dug up again?" Amelia wondered what reason anyone would have for doing that.

"Yeah, possibly. I'll need to take some samples of the dirt in her hair and clothes."

The pathologist stood up. Janine Turnball had worked with West Midlands Police for at least twenty years and would have met Chloe at other crime scenes. Concern for Amelia seemed her priority now though.

"How long would she have been in the ground?"

"Hours. A few days at a push."

"And then?"

"In the freezer? Pretty soon after death would be my guess."

They'd taken her from The Devil's house, buried her, then dug her up and kept her in a freezer somewhere. Someone had planned this, always intending that, at some point, she would be displayed like the other dead women — a carcass of little use to them other than as a trophy, like the skin of a lion or the head of a deer.

Amelia didn't need to ask how her friend had died. She'd witnessed the fatal shot to the head at close range. That memory had played on a reel in her head for many nights. Now she knew this scene would. They didn't need to catch the killer — Michal had seen to that. But they would at least be able to give some peace to her family.

"Stop!"

Amelia turned just in time to prevent Dion, Chloe's boyfriend, from entering the tent behind her. She pushed him back outside as forcibly as she could. "You don't want to see her."

Dion grabbed his hair in his hands and screamed. "It's her, then?"

A quiet, "Yes" was all that was needed.

His eyes sought Amelia's. "That's good. I've missed her."

It seemed a strange thing to say but Amelia understood the sentiment. She'd missed Chloe, too. Sod the COVID regulations and the current situation! Amelia pulled Dion into a hug as she would her own child.

They stood like that, undisturbed by the other members of the force who were carrying out their duties around them, giving them the time and space to grieve. Chloe was one of their own. Fortunately, no press had arrived yet and there were no civilian onlookers to see the reality of a police death.

A few moments later, Amelia pulled away. "We need to go and tell Chloe's parents."

Dion nodded. "I'll come with you."

Amelia led him to her car. They could sort out Dion's car later. Maybe one of the officers would drive it back to Dion's house.

It wasn't far to Chloe's parents' place. They lived just off the A45 in the village of Allesley. Dion didn't say a word on the half-hour journey. Nor did Amelia.

Chloe's mum, Hannah, must have seen them pull up. She opened the front door before they walked up the path. She knew, of course. She knew what they were about to say. Why else would they both be coming to the house?

"You've found Chloe."

Chloe's father stood behind his wife in the doorway and shrieked, steadying himself by grabbing the doorframe. Amelia had imagined it would be the other way around, that Chloe's dad would be calm, while her mum would break.

Dion took charge, leading them both to the lounge while Amelia made tea. Opening and closing cupboards, searching for mugs and tea bags steadied her so she could face the inevitable questions. *What would she want to know if it was one of her children?*

Amelia carried the tray of teas into the lounge. She'd made Dion and herself one, despite not usually drinking the brew. The first thing that struck her about the living room was the number of photographs. They covered the walls and any table or shelf space. They were all of Chloe with her mum and dad. They didn't have any other children. Amelia had discovered this when she first met them a couple of weeks after her murder. She hadn't been able to face them until then. Amelia didn't remember a room full of memories. These photographs had been added as a reminder of her life.

On the table next to Amelia were pictures from Chloe's police graduation ceremony, wearing her freshly-pressed uniform and the flat policewoman's hat. Some people on the force could almost name the exact year of each ceremony from the uniforms the graduates wore. But it wasn't the uniform that Chloe wore that struck Amelia — it was her hair. The flat, short cut made her look even younger than she was and gave her a tomboyish air. Even though Chloe was smiling in the photo, she was not yet the assured, independent and individual woman that Amelia remembered.

Amelia was so busy staring at the photos that she missed Hannah's first question.

"Can we see her?" Hannah repeated.

Dion didn't answer. Maybe he was considering whether he looked less of a boyfriend by not asking the same.

Amelia cleared her throat. "I'd always advise that, after a long period since death, it's best that you remember Chloe as she was."

Hannah persisted, "But I want to see her. I need to see her."

Often, after such a long period, the dead would look nothing like the person. This wasn't the case. Chloe would be recognisable, and Hannah had every right to see her daughter.

"I'll arrange it for you." Amelia stood, planning to call the mortuary from the kitchen.

"I don't want to see her." It was little more than a mumble, but Chloe's father made himself clear. He stood and left the room, pushing past Amelia without looking in her direction.

"He likes to think she's still here." Hannah gestured to the photos.

Amelia arrived home an hour later. Her plan was to shower, change her clothes and head to the office. Her team would need her around right now, particularly Will and those who had known Chloe. She needed to be seen but, more importantly, she needed to work.

Instead, she reached for her phone and dialled Michal's number. He answered on the third ring with a breathless, "You okay?"

"We found Chloe."

"Where are you?"

"At home, but don't come. I'm going to the office."

"Amelia —"

"I'm okay." She looked to the floor, noticing the crumbs from one of Callum's biscuits on the carpet.

"No, Amelia, you're not."

She almost said, "I don't need you," but stopped herself short. "I'll come to see you later if that's okay?"

"Of course. I'll go home and wait for you."

He was at the boxing club, probably training. She'd disturbed him.

"I... appreciate that."

She needed him — or someone. She didn't say anything to Jola, who looked at her quizzically as she passed her in the hall to leave the house only twenty minutes after she arrived. She didn't want to have to say it again. *We've found Chloe.*

Back at the station, Pat had prepared one of the meeting rooms for a debrief. Coffee and a variety of cakes were set up on one of the tables. Amelia wasn't in the least bit hungry, but she poured herself a coffee and sat at one of the tables. She'd washed her face before entering the room, not wanting to display her emotions too openly. Raw was how she felt, both inside and out.

Pat drew them all to attention. She had obviously prepared a speech. Amelia wondered if they'd covered this in her training: what to do if a member of your team is killed, in bullet points. But of course, Chloe had been killed two and a half years ago. They just didn't have a body to grieve over until now.

Amelia tuned into what Pat was saying. "... there will be a memorial service at some point and, of course, a funeral, though, we do need to be prepared for it not following normal arrangements."

Will coughed. "What do you mean?"

"With the pandemic, we don't know what the new normal will be."

Amelia stood up. "Well, she'll have a full send-off. For her parents and —" she scanned the room, "— colleagues."

Pat paused. "We don't know that. There could be restrictions on numbers."

"I don't fucking care —"

"Amelia. I know she was your partner, but please —"

"Please what? Go along with this shit? Chloe died in the line of duty..." She sat down before her legs failed and she nearly said *in front of my very eyes.*

"I know how you're all feeling." Pat tried to take back control of the room. "And I feel the same. I truly do."

Some of the team nodded. Will just stared at the table. He had known Chloe. Many of the others had not.

"Just to be clear, I've made the murder investigation team aware that we wish to work in partnership with them."

"I'll send them all the files." Will stood up to leave.

Amelia guessed that he'd had enough of this charade, too. How could they not care enough to give her a proper send off, pandemic or no pandemic?

"Thanks, Will. I'm sure they have most of them as her death has been an open case, as you know, but it's best to cover everything."

"We don't know yet who's placing them." Amelia needed to point that out. This wasn't over just because her murderer was dead and couldn't be brought to justice.

"Exactly," Pat smiled. "We don't know who's placing the bodies of the women who died at the hands of this particular OCG."

"They're clearly still operating in some capacity." Talking in terms of her job made it easier. Work would get her through this.

"The OCG? You're right. Are they still operating through Europe? Has someone else taken over, or is this just the remnants of the gang finishing off the loose ends?"

Amelia stared at Pat. She wanted her to be clear and precise on what their role was going forward. "So we can investigate this?"

"It's never been closed, Amelia. This OCG is still operating, so we must act. I know you have other cases and assignments, but we must keep this investigation on the go. It can't be your only priority, but we do need to find out who's behind the laying out and storage of the women these men killed, and if they're still operating as a trafficking gang. Or is this them simply completing the work started by the Devil?"

Completing their work. Finishing off what they started. It seemed so clinical, but maybe that was the point — one or two individuals completing the tasks they'd been given. But why now? If they had Chloe all this time, then why dispose of her body now? And why display her in that way?

The other officers in the room had taken their cakes and coffee and gone back to their desks, leaving only Catherine and Amelia in the room.

Catherine read her colleague's mood. "It's odd, isn't it?"

"Sorry?"

"Chloe being left at a scene like that, now."

"He's playing us."

"Who is?"

"Whoever's placing the bodies. He's kept them refrigerated somewhere and now he's leaving them to be found."

"You mean like an undertaker. He's getting them ready to be buried."

Maybe that was his role. The women died for whatever reason — they were getting too angry or difficult or they simply got in the way and their killer was a sadist — then someone took them away to deal with their bodies at a later date.

So why not just bury them or incinerate them in some way? Why wait until now to place them in different locations? Unless, of course, this "undertaker" got some enjoyment out of it.

Chapter 14

Aftermath

Amelia woke on Saturday with a fuzzy head. It took her a few moments to realise that she wasn't at home. Michal lay softly snoring beside her, his arm across her stomach. She gently lifted it off and sat up.

It wasn't a move that she regretted in any way. It was good that they'd managed to cross the gulf between them. They hadn't talked about The Devil or Chloe at dinner. Instead, they'd discussed far happier and mundane topics – Callum's obsession with dinosaurs and trucks, Caitlyn's boxing and Becky's university plans, which changed daily.

Amelia decided to make coffee and toast. She wasn't on duty today and Pat had made it clear that she had to take some downtime or she would suspend her. Amelia could, by rights, take some compassionate leave and see a therapist, but that wasn't her usual style. Normally, she'd work herself to death, avoiding staying still, which would allow negative thoughts to consume her.

She found some croissants in the bread bin so she heated those instead and added butter and jam to the tray. While Amelia was considering whether it was sensible to eat these in bed, she didn't notice that Michal had woken and was standing behind her. She jumped as she felt his arms encircle her waist and his head rest on her shoulders.

"Breakfast. Thanks, I'm famished." Michal lifted one of the croissants off the plate and stuffed half of it in his mouth, oblivious of the crumbs settling in his chest hair. He was, at least, wearing jogging bottoms or she might not have been able to concentrate on breakfast.

Amelia smiled. "Let's at least sit down at the table."

Amelia was still grinning to herself as she drove home. Last night, she'd rung her mother like an errant teenager to tell her that she wouldn't be home. Of course, there were no admonishments, just a brief, "Enjoy!"

Her kids wouldn't say anything as they'd just think she'd been working, though she expected them to be pleased that she was back on solid ground with Michal — when and if she told them. They seemed to like him, particularly Caitlyn, of course. He was her mentor and trainer, and definitely one of the good guys.

Her mum had the news on when she got home. The figures displayed were significant. The death rate from the virus was rising, with over twenty now reported and over a thousand reported cases. In other countries, the numbers of cases and deaths were far higher. Many of her colleagues were starting new roles on Monday.

"They'll be locking me up, soon." Jane dropped her knitting into her lap and scowled.

"Don't be so bloody ridiculous."

"You've not been listening to the news. It'll be the schools next, you watch."

"Schools?"

"Yeah. They'll be shutting them." Her mum shook a knitting needle at her. "You'd better tell Jola that she'll need to be a teacher as well as a childminder, cook and cleaner from now on."

Thanks, Mum. As if I don't feel guilty enough. But, of course, she knew all this was coming. Why else would they be moving so many staff to digital intelligence? Even the admins had been told they could now work at home. Her mind was elsewhere, though, understandably.

Jola chose that moment to enter the room with Callum following behind her. He ran up to Amelia and jumped on her lap. She leaned forward and hugged him.

"Did you have a good night?" Jola smirked. Callum started to squirm then dropped to the floor. Amelia blushed and didn't answer. "I'll take that as a yes. I'm pleased for you."

Amelia's mother tutted.

"Well done, both of you. You've made me feel like a teenager and not a grown woman." Amelia stood, nearly treading on her son. "I'll leave you both to it."

"Amelia, sit down. We're only teasing you." Jane picked up the remote and turned off the television.

She was about to start knitting again when Jola interjected, "Why don't we all go for a walk?"

A walk? That's what normal families did on a Saturday morning.

"Dinner's in the slow cooker and we've got an hour before I need to do anything else. I'm sure the girls won't mind." Jola's shiny enthusiasm wasn't rubbing off.

Jane stared at Amelia, waiting for a response, no doubt expecting the usual reply, "You all go. I've got to work." Instead, Amelia smiled and said, "Why not? I'll find the girls."

They were both in their rooms and were up and dressed so they were all ready to leave the house in minutes.

Memorial Park was heaving. Everyone in

the local area must have had the same idea. At least they hadn't come by car as the car park was full and wardens were slapping tickets on all the vehicles parked on nearby verges. It wasn't even particularly sunny. Low, grey clouds hung ominously above them, threatening persistent rain, but no one seemed to care. It felt like they were all trying to absorb as much fresh air as possible before that small luxury was removed. Most of the people walking in the park were either young families with a trail of children or older people with scarves over their mouths despite it not being that cold for mid-March.

"Better make the most of it before prison looms."

Amelia never felt so relieved that she would always be working — would always be a critical worker. To be shut inside with her family was her worst nightmare.

Callum ran towards the swings. Jola chased after him, leaving Amelia wondering what Jola would do when he reached the crowded play area. She didn't stop him and queued behind a mother and child waiting for a free swing. Amelia was torn. Leave them be, or interject? She chose to let them carry on. A few minutes later, she joined them as it was Callum's turn to fly high on the toddler swing. His laughter was infectious.

Caitlyn had brought her skateboard and disappeared to the skate park. Her sister sat on a nearby bench with Jane and took a book out of her bag to read. Amelia hoped it was a proper book, not another of her textbooks. She was proud of her studious daughter but, apart from spending time with her boyfriend, all she seemed to do these days was revise.

Callum had moved onto the climbing frame

and Amelia spotted a familiar figure walking towards them.

"Are you stalking me?"

Michal grinned. "Caitlyn told me you were here."

If Amelia thought it was odd that her ten-year-old daughter was messaging Michal, she didn't show it. Maybe they'd arranged a coaching session and she'd had to cancel.

Michal took over toddler watch so Jola and Amelia could join the others watching from the bench. Callum threw himself at a pole, grabbing it just in time and swirling around it with the enthusiasm that only a toddler could have.

Amelia exhaled and turned to Jola. "Is he always that brave?"

"You should see him on the pyramid."

The pyramid was a tall structure of ropes that Callum would have needed to be lifted to reach. Amelia shut her eyes and silently wondered how it was that her son had not yet needed a trip to the casualty department. He came rushing over at that point shouting, "Ice cream!"

They left Caitlyn happily skateboarding and headed to the café. No one thought of denying him the pleasure of an ice cream despite it being nearly lunchtime. It was that type of day when anything goes, like a day trip to the seaside. Michal took Amelia's hand, causing her daughter to wink at her.

The idyllic family day out had to come to an end at some point. Amelia felt her phone vibrate in her pocket. She waved everyone on with a brief, "I'll catch you up." She turned away from them. "DI Barton."

"Hi Amelia, it's Will." Even though Amelia was Will's superior, they never used official titles. He should call her Ma'am, but the intelligence officer had worked with Amelia long enough to know that she would treat that with disdain.

"What's up?"

"We've had reports of men being bundled into a van at the site of your ops warehouse."

It probably meant that they were moving on. She could kick herself that she'd left the car at home. "I'll get over there as soon as I can. The others on the op can probably get there before me."

"I'm on it."

Instead of catching her family up, Amelia simply texted Michal. GOTTA RUN. WORK NEEDS ME. SPEAK SOON. TELL THE OTHERS. x

Amelia was fit but hated jogging. At least she was wearing trainers.

Three-quarters of an hour later, after speeding up the A45, Amelia arrived at the boat. Sean and Catherine were already there. They'd set up surveillance in the back cabin.

Catherine spotted Amelia first. "Looks like they've taken the men from the warehouse to another location. The women are still here but look distressed."

"Anyone on the men?"

Sean answered, "No. The reports from the public were followed up by the local force but, by that time, they'd gone."

"I'm guessing they've decided to move the men to other jobs rather than get them stuck here after lockdown."

Amelia stared at the scene on the screen in front of her. It wasn't surprising that some of the women had hidden themselves on their mattresses under the thin sheets they'd been provided with. They must be petrified that they'd be taken next.

"What d'you reckon, boss? They going to move the women on, too?"

It was possible that they'd look for another location to set up a brothel. Their nail bar days were probably over but their captors would still want to make money from them. Punters would still pay for sex either by video or in person — both, while they could get away with it, Amelia guessed. Keeping them here made as much sense as moving them.

"I reckon they'll keep them here for now, but we need to be aware that they could be moved at any time. I know we're not supposed to be on 24-hour surveillance. I'll see if we can get local police back up."

"How else do we keep the women safe?" Catherine sighed.

Quite, thought Amelia. Her phone pinged. Will had sent a video. Sean put it up on one of the computer screens so that she could share it with her colleagues.

"Will says it's from a member of the public who filmed the men being bundled into the van."

"That was careless of them. Why not sneak them out at night? Why take the risk?"

The video began with a shot of two men grabbing the shoulders of a smaller man, possibly Vietnamese. They had him in a shoulder lock and were pushing him towards the doors of a large, white van. He was refusing to move his legs, which meant they were trying to support his limp body. The anger on the aggressors' faces was clear. But to his credit, their smaller captive wasn't giving up as they now dragged him, his feet tucked under him as he stayed limp, towards the van.

The next shot showed the inside of the

van where approximately ten other men were sitting on the floor. They weren't struggling or shackled in any way. They were just resigned, staring into space.

One of the gang-masters was recognisable. The other kept his face down the whole time. Amelia wasn't surprised to see Cheun. Nor was she surprised to see how brazen he was. He was just asking to be taken in.

The video stopped abruptly. Maybe the illicit cameraman had been spotted. Maybe he'd decided to sneak away to ring the police.

Amelia left the others to watch the video again. She went to the dinette, sat down and rang Pat's number. She needed her agreement to raid Cheun's home and bring him in. Instead of immediately agreeing, Pat asked Amelia to stop by at WMROC.

It had started to rain by the time Amelia pulled up at the office block. She imagined her family sitting around the dining table eating their chicken casserole. No doubt Michal had been invited to join them. Her plate of food would be covered with foil, ready to be heated in the microwave on her return. Covering her head with her handbag, Amelia made a dash for the entrance.

Amelia spotted Will at his desk. He was hunched over his laptop. "Thanks."

He looked up and smiled. "Always a pleasure to pass on a lead."

"Thought you'd be at home since we're not being paid for weekends."

"It's quieter here."

She'd heard on the grapevine that he was having a few marital issues, but who wasn't? At least he didn't have three kids at home.

Amelia gestured towards Pat's office.

"Any idea what she wants?"

"Your head on a stick?" Will grinned. "No idea. But she does have a visitor with her."

As if on cue, Amelia heard a sharp sigh behind her. "We haven't got all day."

"I've been summoned," Amelia whispered to Will.

Pat did, indeed, have a visitor. A bald, Chinese man in a suit sat in one of the comfier chairs in Pat's office, brushing lint off his trouser.

"This is Dr Mo. He's a leading academic on Chinese and South Asian gangs."

Amelia held out her hand. Dr Mo just waved it away.

"Amelia, we're in the middle of a pandemic."

"Sorry," she muttered. "I thought we were going to discuss arresting the operative we've identified.'

"Lee Cheun?" Dr Mo had clearly been kept abreast of the day's events.

Amelia nodded. "Is he known to you?"

"Bottom rung." Dr Mo was clearly a man of few words, not common in an academic.

Pat tapped her pencil on her desk. "So you know of him?"

"Yes, he's a lowly member of the Midlands Dragons, an OCG that operates across the region. There are many layers of the group that obviously link back to OCGs in China and Hong Kong."

"What's their main line of business?" Amelia pulled a chair closer to the so-called expert, wondering why, since he knew so much, he hadn't dobbed in the entire Midlands Triad. Maybe he had and there was never enough evidence to charge them?

Dr Mo pursed his lips. He looked bored.

"Trafficking. Drugs and people — the usual in these modern times."

"Sex trafficking?"

"Women are trafficked for both commercial and sexual reasons. They'll use them in brothels but also to help launder money through businesses such as nail bars."

For fuck's sake, tell us something we don't already know! Amelia looked to her boss for support.

"I've spoken to Dr Mo and we don't think it's a good idea to pick up Lee Cheun yet." Pat didn't look directly at Amelia. "We'll set up a unit to monitor his movements."

Nice to be consulted on my own operation. "But I thought we didn't have the resources for 24/7 on the warehouse."

"We don't. We'll use local detectives to follow Cheun. It won't cover the whole period, but it'll give us a snapshot of his whereabouts."

Amelia didn't bother to ask about the safety of the trafficked women and men. There was little point, as the whole operation was clearly such a low priority. Perhaps they should just dump them all in the canal and have done with it. This was a waste of time.

She turned to Dr Mo. "Do you have a number I can call you on?"

He opened his jacket, reached for his inside pocket and handed her a card. Amelia wondered how much the university was paying this expert. She'd have got as much detail from wiki.

Pat didn't look up as Amelia stormed out of the office, waving to Will as she left. If she was lucky, she might get home before Michal gave up on her.

As she got in her car, a text came through from her friend and colleague, Carol: PUB.

She didn't need to ask where. Instead, she immediately drove towards The Shepherd.

DCI Carol Jamieson had joined the police in the same year as Amelia. Their paths had crossed many times and they had become good friends over the years. Carol worked as a senior officer in the Public Protection Unit. She supported the most vulnerable in sex and domestic abuse cases, amongst other roles. She was tough and not the mumsy figure you might expect in this role.

Carol was at the bar when Amelia entered the back room. She was surprised to see that Shiv had joined them. Siobhan Grady ran Poppy's Place, a refuge for women fleeing sex work and trafficking. She seemed to be in just the mood for a stiff drink as she grabbed the whiskey from Carol and took a healthy slug.

"Bloody council." Shiv never minced her words when it came to bureaucracy.

"Why? What's happened?" Amelia asked.

"Their stupid, fucking rules when it comes to this flu thing!" Shiv took another slug. "Twenty fucking pages of them... only one woman to a room, limited sharing of bathrooms, regular cleaning… PP fucking E."

Carol raised her eyebrows. "I can see how that might be an issue."

"A fucking issue? It's the women. Do they think the numbers in need will drop if we're all locked down?"

"They'll go up." Amelia knew this, as did her friends.

"Exactly." Shiv slammed her empty glass down on the table. Carol rose to get her another. "They'll be locked up with their pimps and little fucking work. How long do they think it'll be before they're at my door with bruises? And what am I supposed to say? Sorry, there's no room at the inn?"

The landlord took the empty glass from Carol. "Shall I just line them up?"

Carol raised her pint of brown ale. "Please."

The landlord gestured Carol closer. "I'll keep the back room open just for the police during lockdown."

Carol winked at him. "I didn't hear that."

He carried on wiping glasses with his mucky tea towel. At least the beer he served was strong enough to counter germs.

Amelia decided to try and change the subject and let Siobhan calm down for a few minutes. She turned to Carol. "How's work?"

"Busy. We've got a load of Place of Safety Orders to enact. And..." she turned to Shiv, "loads of red tape to get past — so you're not the only one who's fuming."

There was a comfortable silence. Amelia scanned the familiar surroundings of the backroom. It lacked a good focal point like a roaring fire. The solitary milk churn next to the bar just wasn't cutting it.

Carol took a long gulp of ale. "We've heard about Chloe. You okay, mate?"

So now they were getting to the real reason for the pub meetup. She'd done it for the other two, so she should have expected an intervention, though interventions seemed to be common for her, which was worrying.

Was she okay? "Yeah, I'm good. I guess it gives her mum and dad some finality."

Carol nodded. "A body to bury."

"Exactly."

Shiv shuddered. "Did you see her? Her body, I mean."

"Yeah. They called me to the scene."

Carol half raised her glass. "They shouldn't have done that."

"Why?" Amelia felt affronted. "It's part of my case."

She was your partner, Amelia. They should have protected you from that.

"I managed to stop Dion from seeing her. That would've been far worse. Maybe I needed some closure, too."

Shiv added her thoughts. "It must have been dreadful. I can't even imagine. But you'll never get closure from the bastard that did it."

Carol suddenly grinned. "How's Michal, by the way?"

Are there no secrets? Maybe she should go and find out if he was still hanging out at hers.

The next morning started with a bang. Caitlyn roared into her bedroom. Fortunately, Michal hadn't stayed over. "There's stuff on the radio about schools being shut! Won't that be great?"

Chapter 15

Lockdown

Amelia was bombarded by a flurry of urgent emails with links to training courses and new strategic operations. Everyone on the logistics teams seemed to think that they were the world's new experts on operating in a pandemic. They had clearly been given orders by their bosses to rethink all tasks relating to major operations in the NCA. There were briefings and training presentations entitled, for example, How to Make a Safe and Successful Arrest. Every single one of these was marked as mandatory training to be completed by an arbitrary date not too far in the distant future.

They could at least have discussed this between them. Amelia totted up the hours they deemed necessary for each course, only to discover that it would add forty hours to the following week's work. By this point, she'd had enough. She reached for her phone and dialled Pat's number. Engaged. It was the same at every attempt for the next thirty minutes. There was nothing else for it. The first email she had that morning suggested that they should work at home when it wasn't strictly necessary for them to work from the office. *Fuck that!* Amelia needed to let off some steam and that needed to be done face to face.

She was stopped in her tracks when she arrived at WMROC. Her usual entry point — a side door that led to the stairs to her floor — had a large sign on it: NO ENTRY. USE RECEPTION. The door keypad had been disconnected, so she couldn't even sneak in this way if she wanted.

At the front door were more new signs. WEAR A FACE MASK. KEEP 2M APART. Once she got into the building using the intercom system, she was instructed to follow the bright yellow arrows on the floor and stand on the large circles at 2m intervals leading to the reception desk. Amelia recognised one of her least favourite receptionists at the front desk, despite her face being covered with both a face mask and shield. It was in the eyes. No one else scowled at her like that.

"I see you didn't study the building map you were sent."

Amelia was tempted to repeat that back to her in a childish parody but, instead, she bit her lip. "I'm assuming I can use the lift up to my floor."

"You need to wear a face mask or you're not going anywhere but back out the front door." The receptionist stared at the monitor in front of her. Amelia wasn't even worth a glance.

Fortunately, Amelia remembered that she had a large packet of new face masks in her rucksack. So, this was their purpose. She opened the bag, found the packet, which she opened with her teeth, pulled one of the masks out by the strap and put the mask on. This was a little more awkward than she expected. She'd tied her long auburn hair back in a tight plait that morning but the strap still kept slipping off her ear.

The receptionist tutted loudly enough for it to be audible to anyone in the reception area.

Amelia gave her a long stare until she felt uncomfortable enough to say, "You can go up now."

"Ma'am."

"Sorry?"

"You can go up now, *ma'am*." Amelia never expected civvies to call her "ma'am" or "boss". She specifically told her team not to. But this occasion demanded it.

Pat was the only person in the NCA office. She was standing at the coffee urn when Amelia entered. This was unusual in itself, as she normally used the coffee machine in her office.

Pat greeted her with, "I ran out of pods."

Amelia nodded and removed her mask, then stepped back when her boss visibly flinched. "I forgot. Sorry."

"New ways of working."

"Yeah, which is sort of why I'm here."

Pat gestured with her mug. "This is the trial run day. All the staff are at home and we've had maintenance in over the weekend sorting out the signage. Didn't you get the email?"

"Which bloody one!?"

"Well, quite." Pat had the grace to grin.

Amelia took the opportunity to make herself a coffee. "Do we have to drink this a special way now?"

"Well, actually…" Pat pointed to another laminated sign. It stated: USE YOUR OWN MUG. DO NOT SOCIALISE IN THE KITCHEN AREA. CLEAN THE WORKSPACE AFTER USE.

Amelia picked up the dishcloth and rinsed it before wiping the work surface. "One out of three isn't bad."

She'd come to bemoan the absurdity of the

new orders but, the longer she stayed in the office, the more uneasy she felt. Maybe she should have paid more attention to the news and her emails. This level of change wouldn't have been put in place without good reason.

Pat must have sensed the change. "I had an email this morning about a full lockdown. It'd be good to run it by you while you're here."

This was the first time that Amelia could remember Pat trusting her as a colleague, seeing her, perhaps, as the next in line in the department. There were other DIs, but their roles were far more office-based. Amelia held the highest rank in the field on current operations. Pat joined them on raids, but Amelia was in charge of her operations on a daily basis. DCI-level officers were becoming overseers.

Amelia sat in Pat's office as her boss outlined what lockdown would mean for the whole community and not just the force. Caitlyn had been right. In the next couple of days, school closures would be announced.

"Your kids can still attend, though." Pat tapped her computer screen with a pen.

"What do you mean?"

"It says here that children of frontline workers will have a place in school if they wish."

Did she want her kids to continue in school? "I'll need to think about it. I've got Jola, and then there's my mum."

Pat paused and glanced at Amelia. "Is she okay now? I guess she's classed as clinically vulnerable."

"I wouldn't call her that to her face." Amelia knew that her mum was more than likely to be on the shielded list. It was only a couple of years ago that she'd had a stroke. That settled it. Her kids would stay at home and Jola would have more work to do. She made a mental note to discuss that with her as soon as she got home.

At some point while Amelia was musing over the effects on her family, Pat had switched off her computer monitor and opened her notebook. "Amelia, I know this is going to be really difficult for our frontline staff like your team. But I have a duty of care to you which is why we've put so many guidelines and training in place for you all. Have you looked at them? That's why I suggested we all work from home today and have a full briefing tomorrow on Teams."

"Teams?"

Pat tutted. "I knew this would happen. Everyone's decided that their task is the most important and now no one will have the basics set up. Help me out here, Amelia. Let's plan what you, as a frontline operative, need to have in place. Then we can brief our colleagues on what's important."

Amelia and Pat spent the next few hours prioritising the information and training that they needed to get ready. As they got stuck into which workstream was important, Amelia began to see the point of the process and, to her surprise, began to enjoy working closely with Pat, who, on more than one occasion, let out a stream of expletives at the arrogance of some guy in IT or Training's micro-managing emails.

Amelia decided by four in the afternoon that her next priority was briefing her team on how to move forward with their operation.

There were few of them left. Catherine had moved to CEOP, which was both a blessing and a curse — a blessing for Catherine as it meant that she could follow up on tracing her niece whilst supposedly working, and a blessing for Amelia as she didn't have a distracted DS on her hands. But the small numbers now involved meant that Amelia was becoming more concerned by the day for the women in the warehouse.

This was further complicated by reports of local homeless support teams travelling around Birmingham, collecting up those without shelter and providing them with accommodation. Local hotels and hostels had been taken over to ensure their safety during the pandemic, and yet a group of trafficked, enslaved women was being left in a warehouse without any heating or access to hot water.

From the recent surveillance reports, it was clear that those women were still being forced to service punters. Surely their safety was as important as everyone else's? Amelia used her newfound knowledge of video conferencing and set up a meeting for all her staff for the next afternoon. She wondered if they'd even notice the invitation in their overflowing inboxes, but there was an all-hands call with Pat that morning for them to practice with.

Amelia returned home with a heavy heart. Jola was cooking tea, her girls were at the kitchen table finishing off their homework, and her mum was playing with Callum. He brought her one of his many hundred dinosaurs and she told him what it was called. Listening to him then trying to pronounce the name was hilarious and Amelia could have sat and watched them all night, but she had to get things sorted here, too.

"Can we all get together when Callum's in bed? We need to sort a few things to do with this bloody virus."

Jola didn't look up from mashing the potatoes. "I know. We all watched that Bojo clown's briefing this morning."

Amelia pulled up the news headlines on her phone just so she could catch up with the news her family already knew. The Prime Minister had announced a full lockdown from the following week but, as yet, not the lockdown of schools. That was to come.

They ate in silence except for Callum, who jabbered on about his dinosaurs non-stop for half an hour.

As soon as he went to bed, they all reconvened at the kitchen table.

Amelia took a deep breath. "Now, you mustn't tell your friends. They'll know in a day or so and it's not going to be a surprise. Schools are shutting."

Caitlyn raised her arms and cheered, "Hooray!"

Jola glared at her.

"Actually, Caitlyn, you could still go to school." Amelia watched her younger daughter's face fall. "But I think, to help your nan out, it might be better if you didn't."

Her mother harrumphed. "I'm fine, thank you very much."

"What about my exams?" Becky sat forward at the table, lines creasing her forehead.

Amelia hadn't thought about this. Becky's AS levels were only a few months away. "I'm not sure. Your teachers will brief you, I expect. Do you want to be in school? With my job —"

"I don't want preferential treatment because you're in the police. My friends won't get that."

Most of her friends' parents ran their own businesses or were office-based. Her daughter was right. They'd stay at home.

"I know it's a lot to ask you both," Amelia looked at her mother and Jola, "watching them and all that."

Jola smiled. "I already help with their homework and they can help with Callum. We'll be fine, won't we, girls?"

They both nodded.

Amelia reached into her handbag hanging on the side of the chair. She got out her purse and handed Jola her credit card. "There might be extra stuff they need. Just order it."

"We can't share a laptop." Becky looked at her sister, as sensible as ever. "Let Caitlyn have a new one. All my work's on mine."

As Caitlyn's face lit up, Jola brought her straight back to earth. "She can use the iPad."

"Get her a reconditioned laptop just in case. Do we need anything else?"

"Can I have some revision books?"

Amelia sighed. She wanted her daughter to do well, but she needed a break, too. "What about some downtime? You could learn a new skill —"

Becky stood up. "I've got exams..."

Amelia watched her daughter as she left the room, thinking how unlikely that probably was. This crisis wasn't going away in a couple of weeks. Was she the only one that had come to that conclusion?

Caitlyn was chewing her bottom lip. "What about my boxing lessons? That man said we can't meet people outside of work or school."

For the first time Amelia thought — *what about Michal?*

Amelia considered ringing Michal that evening as she watched some of the ridiculous training videos. She even considered inviting him over so she could practice the restraint and arrest holds that they proposed for future use. This would have been amusing if it wasn't so ridiculous. She hadn't considered it before, but it was more than likely that some low-life would employ spitting now as their main line of defence against arrest. She hadn't discussed it with Pat that morning, but she was more than aware that all frontline workers would be at risk of catching the virus and there was no way of mitigating that. They couldn't don full PPE before arresting a suspect! She'd seen videos of staff in hospitals wearing gowns, gloves, masks and shields. They'd been given some of these, but if the public were at risk or if they'd just chased down a suspect then, of course, they weren't going to waste minutes and miss losing them by taking time to put on protective gear.

Maybe she should move out? She could move onto the boat, at least. That would bring the dual advantages of round-the-clock surveillance and also minimise the risk of her bringing the virus home to her family.

She messaged Michal. I'M THINKING OF LIVING APART FROM EVERYONE. DON'T WANT TO KILL YOU ALL.

Her phone lit up. He was trying to ring her. She ignored it. A few seconds later, he replied to her text. COME AND LIVE HERE IF YOU NEED

126

TO.

They'd only just got back together… that was bound to kill off the relationship. She ignored him, figuring that the message required more thought than she had the capacity to give. Maybe she'd chat to some other officers with families first, to see what they were doing.

Just before midnight, she was dragged back from training video hell by a message from Sean. NEED YOU AT THE BOAT.

Chapter 16
At Risk

Amelia arrived at the boat expecting to see some signs of activity, but all was quiet. She knocked on the wooden doors in the well deck before opening them. She didn't want to startle Sean. He was sitting at the laptop, intently watching the screen, and only glanced up when Amelia stepped into the boat.

"What's the emergency?" If Amelia had been expecting more of a sense of panic, then she didn't show it.

"I needed a woman." Amelia blinked and he grinned. "Not like that. I need a female officer. One of the trafficked women is washing her clothes in the canal just up by the next bridge. I just thought it would be a good opportunity to speak to her."

Washing her clothes in the canal. Amelia let that sink in. She wouldn't let a dog swim in the canal water or even clean the boat with it. She certainly wouldn't expect anyone to be washing in it, but then, what choice did the women have?

"Good call, Sean. I'll pop out and see if she's still there."

As soon as she left the boat and glanced up towards the bridge, Amelia noticed a faint light. She'd walked up from the car park in the opposite direction and hadn't noticed it earlier. She heard the splashing before making out the shape of the small woman kneeling under the bridge. The woman looked up when she heard Amelia's approach and nearly dropped the small torch that she held in her mouth into the cut. Amelia recognised her then. It was Julie.

Neither woman spoke for a moment. Julie took her torch out of her mouth and placed it on top of the wet clothes that were now in a plastic bucket on the side of the canal. Amelia could make out a ring of soapy bubbles drifting away from the towpath towards the centre of the canal in the faint light emanating from the torch.

Julie didn't move, which Amelia took as a good sign. "I saw the torchlight from our boat. I thought it might just be a night fisherman but I'm on my own tonight and wanted to check."

Julie didn't reply. She sat statuesque, staring at the other side of the bridge. Maybe she was hoping that Amelia would just leave her alone, knowing that she wasn't a threat.

"Look, Julie. We both know this isn't normal. Do you want to explain? Are you homeless? Can I help?"

Julie folded her arms and hugged her knees. She was now leaning against the wall of the bridge. Amelia sat down next to her, forgetting that she was supposed to be sitting two metres away.

Julie coughed. Amelia shuffled away.

"I'm okay. But some of my friends..." Julie tailed off, perhaps knowing that she'd said too much.

"Your friends — are they ill?"

Julie looked at Amelia then. Amelia noticed how smooth her skin was. When they'd spoken before, she'd looked much older, with tense, tight features that strained when she spoke. Tonight she seemed as calm as the still water next to her. "Some. Not all. They have a cough and they're hot."

Amelia had to call this in. They couldn't

risk these women's lives any longer. "Where do you live?"

She knew the answer, of course, but she couldn't tell Julie that she'd been watching her and her friends for weeks.

Julie stood and grabbed the bucket, forgetting the torch, which skidded off into the water. She quickly placed the bucket under her arm and sprinted off. Amelia could have run and caught her, but she knew where she was going.

Back at the boat, Amelia recounted what had been said to Sean. At what point should they prioritise the danger to individuals over the risks of ending an operation? This was always tricky. Amelia always exercised more caution than most of her colleagues but, in this case, there were other factors too, mainly the risk to the public. These women were still working in close proximity with punters. They certainly weren't socially distancing from them and no one would be bothering with face masks.

Sean called Pat. "The risk's too great, surely... I'm not a doctor... Maybe you should ask Amelia..."

She should have called. She reached over for Sean's mobile and recounted again what Julie had told her.

"It could just be a cold."

"And it could be Coronavirus. Do we want an outbreak centred around one of our operations?"

Pat paused. "There may already be one. Leave it with me and I'll speak to the Super."

Amelia had an answer rehearsed but Pat had already ended the call. She turned to Sean. "Let's take a look at the recent footage and see if we can spot who's ill."

Sean wound the footage back about half an hour. Amelia picked out individual women and waited for them to cough or show signs of illness. There were about five women asleep on the mattresses, facing away from the camera and barely moving. Were they ill?

"Rewind the footage to this afternoon."

Sean did as he was asked. The women were in the same place. The rest of the group seemed to be awake at this point. Some were applying make-up and doing their hair. Maybe they'd been chosen to work that night. Amelia spotted Julie collecting clothes from around the sick beds. Maybe she thought that would help. She then started gesticulating towards the other half of the room where the door to the outside staircase was located. They hadn't managed to get a camera up there. Amelia wondered if it was one of the OCG she was gesticulating at. Perhaps they knew they had sick women on their hands and were ignoring them? None of the OCG entered the room. They kept their distance and just used the women they thought were healthy, taking them upstairs to meet their clients. If only these clients knew what a cesspit the women were kept in! But what did they care? They were cheap and available.

At 5:30 in the morning, Amelia gave up waiting for a reply from her boss. The briefing started at 8 am. She might as well go home and use the next hour or two to prepare for her Teams call. Pat's priority would be the safety of her whole staff for now, but she hoped she could catch her after and restate her case.

No one seemed to be competent with the IT. Half the team logged on late and the others sat there either with their cameras or mics off, barely saying anything. It was excruciating for Amelia, who wanted to unmute herself and lay into everyone about the poor health of the captive women. But Pat had messaged her earlier to warn her off. STAY ON THE LINE AT THE END OF THE CALL AND I'LL FILL YOU IN ON WHAT WE PLAN TO DO ABOUT YOUR OP.

The briefing began twenty minutes late. Pat started by saying that she just wanted brief feedback from each team leader and then she'd do some reminders of the operational guidelines they should now be aware of. That was, of course, if they'd read their emails.

Amelia listened to the other reports. They were standard and mostly intelligence-based. The known OCGs in the West Midlands appeared to be hunkering down. There was some expectation that they would change their modus operandi, moving their operations to online. Will reported that they already had intelligence of an upsurge in traffic on the dark web.

When it came to Amelia's turn, she kept it brief. The men had been moved from the factory and the women who remained were no longer working in the nail bar but were still being prostituted in the evenings. She didn't mention their health concerns because she didn't get the chance to. Pat practically cut her off mid-sentence as soon as she'd given the briefest of reports.

Amelia sat drumming her fingers, switching off from the rest of the briefing. Becky came into her office a few minutes later with a coffee for her. There were some

positives about working from home. Her
daughter sat down on the worn couch that
Amelia used to catnap on when work was hectic,
which was most of the time.

"You okay?" Amelia wondered why her
daughter wasn't working.

"I'm scared."

Amelia hadn't thought about the impact
the virus was having. She understood that
people were worried or anxious. The changes
were immense – but *scared*?

"Why's that, love?"

"I'm scared we'll lose Nan. After the
stroke..."

They had to keep her mother safe. If that
meant barricading her in, then so be it, but
it raised other issues. Amelia was frontline
staff, putting her mother at risk every time
she left the house and returned.

"I can stay at a hostel or something."

Becky clasped her hands together. "Oh,
fuck! Mum, I didn't mean that."

Of course, she didn't, but she was still
right. "Don't swear, Becks." Amelia winked.
"Especially when your nan's around."

Becky laughed, relieving some of the
tension.

"Maybe we could look at cleaning and meal
times so I spend less time in the same space,"
Amelia suggested. This was more Becky's
domain.

"Good idea. I'll draw up a plan and run
it by everyone." Becky stood up, went over to
her mum and hugged her. Amelia held onto her
daughter longer than usual, concerned that
this was the last hug she was going to get
from her family for a while.

When Becky left the office, Amelia

reached into her desk drawer and pulled out a large envelope. She opened its flap and spilt the contents onto her desk. Sifting through, she found the photograph she wanted. They were all there, smiling at the camera. Amelia, her mum, her daughters and son, and, of course, Jola. Michal had taken the picture when they were at the beginning of their romance. It was the same one that she had framed on her desk both at home and at work. She'd always meant to keep this smaller version in her purse but just hadn't done it. It seemed appropriate to do so today.

Then she tuned back into the briefing. Pat seemed to be winding up. Her last instruction, "Let's be careful out there," had the older staff grinning. This was followed by, "Stay on, Amelia, if you would."

Neither woman said anything until the other officers had signed off, their names disappearing one at a time.

Then Pat began, "We've sought Public Health advice and feel that the women are young enough to cope with the virus."

Amelia tried to interject but Pat held up her hand. "However, they're likely to be malnourished, so I'm going to suggest that we increase your team back to four so that there's round-the-clock coverage."

Amelia knew that a full surveillance team was at least sixteen strong, but they'd never had that anyway. "Do I get Catherine back?"

"Yes, of course."

There were some positives then.

"Do you want me to draw up the shift patterns?" Amelia smiled. It was a small victory, but there was still the women's health to consider. "What are the protocols if the women fail to improve or more become sick?"

Pat looked away from the camera. "We need to plan an exit strategy. Do you think Cheun will be a viable target?"

What Pat meant was — would he turn and give up information on the wider OCG? Amelia very much doubted it. If they removed the women, Cheun and a few of his foot soldiers would be the only ones they would ever hook. These women might be safe, but they'd just set up a new base from which to operate using other trafficked women and men.

"No, Cheun won't turn." *Might as well be honest.*

"Then you know what we need to do," Pat paused. "It might be worth talking to your mate, Siobhan, to see if there's room at the refuge if we need to place them."

From the last conversation Amelia had with Siobhan, she very much doubted it. More women were seeking help and fewer beds were available. It was probably the case with the Sally Army and other providers of rooms, too. In fact, Coventry had made the move to support those on the streets with accommodation. It was a great move, but it left little for those who also needed the space, like those fleeing domestic abuse. There was always a tug of war for limited resources in times of great need, Amelia hoped that her women wouldn't be the ones to lose out.

Chapter 17
Removal

The Undertaker wrapped the women in black plastic bags pausing only to apply duct tape that he cut with his teeth. Three of them, all of a similar size and shape, tiny and insignificant.

He wore an apron, gloves, mask and face shield. They were barely clothed. No one would even miss them and to him, their undertaker, they were nothing.

He piled the three bodies into the back of the van. He expected to return to the old mill in the days to come. He knew the canal well from his childhood and, if he had the time, he would trace the history of this broken building – but not today while he was performing a job, a job with decent, if irregular, pay that gave him some degree of satisfaction.

Chapter 18
Abandoned

Catherine didn't seem pleased to be reassigned again. She had only spent a week at CEOP, but Amelia understood that she'd been messed around. Catherine stomped around the boat that evening. Barely speaking, she made numerous coffees as an excuse not to look at the screen.

Amelia was concerned, not only for her partner but also because her headcount had come up short. Some of the women were missing and had been for a couple of hours. Amelia had named them all when she started the job. Julie was the only one who had a "real" name and Amelia didn't believe for one minute that it was her true name. Maybe she'd picked it up at the nail bar. It was some of the ill women that were missing. Amelia hoped that was because they'd been moved so that they wouldn't infect the others, but there were more who looked sick now, their thin bedding askew, bodies curled up and only moving when racked with a bout of coughing. She fired off an email to Pat, not hiding her concerns and demanding once again that they step in. She knew this was unlikely to happen.

Catherine appeared not to notice the issue. She sat hugging yet another cup of coffee. When she placed it down on the table next to her, Amelia noticed her shaking hand.

"Have you eaten?"

Catherine sighed, "I was just going to make a sandwich. You want one?"

"Yeah, thanks." Amelia was beginning to feel like a parent to Catherine. She was very much aware of her partner's diabetes and hesitated to draw attention to it, but the last thing she needed was her sergeant in a coma. It was commendable that she hadn't decided to work from home, but if she wasn't going to be helpful, then she may as well have. Perhaps that was what bothered her.

The sandwich arrived moments later. Amelia realised she was quite hungry and tucked into the tuna sandwich on white bread. When she'd finished the first half, she glanced over to her partner, who seemed to just be nibbling at hers.

"What's up?"

Catherine looked up. "Nothing," she mumbled.

Amelia laughed. "You could've fooled me."

Catherine picked another corner off the bread and raised it to her mouth. "I was on to something."

Amelia guessed that she wasn't talking about this case. "With your niece?"

"Yeah."

Working at CEOP gave Catherine more opportunities to find clues about her niece's whereabouts. Amelia got that. There was little she could do other than ask for a different officer to take on the work. It would give Catherine more time, but she'd still be doing unofficial work on NCA time and Amelia doubted that it was her place to support that.

Catherine continued. "I've traced some drug traffic along the route between Weston and Worcestershire."

"It could be linked, I suppose."

"If I can pinpoint where they are, then I can go and look for Aleesha."

"It might not be her."

"They'll have been keeping a low profile over the last week and —"

Amelia stopped eating. "Cath. It could be anyone. Why would they risk moving kids about with the schools shut now?"

Catherine sat forward. She'd thought this through. "But that's the point. Kids on a train journey during the day — with bags. What are people going to think?"

"That they should be isolating at home?"

"But they can still see their estranged parents. That's the law, isn't it?"

Amelia couldn't deny that.

Catherine pursed her lips. "I need to get back to work on CEOP."

Amelia had another idea, one that would both avoid leaving her without support and prevent Catherine from getting into trouble for not completing her assigned tasks with CEOP.

"Why don't I speak with Dion, see if he can assign the search to someone or keep your access up?"

Catherine brightened up. "Would you?"

Amelia rang Dion. He'd returned to active duty the previous day. Amelia scolded him for it. She knew more than many that the grieving process takes months, not days.

"I'd rather work," Dion muttered.

"I thought the same, Dion, but then I made one mistake after another. Fortunately, I had colleagues to support me through it."

"Are you suggesting mine won't?"

Amelia regretted the call. She couldn't offer Dion anything to assuage his grief and now she was going to ask him a favour. "Listen, Dion. Catherine's got a family issue."

"Your DS?"

"Yes." *Chloe's replacement.* Could this get any worse?

"Okay. I'll help if I can."

"Catherine was assigned to CEOP. Her niece is in trouble — county line stuff."

Dion interjected. "It's okay. I know who her niece is."

This could be good or bad. "Then you know that she needs help."

"Can't Catherine access this herself?"

"She's been put back on Operation Caludon." Amelia nearly called it Operation Narrowboat as the other officers jokingly referred to it.

"Ah. I get your issue."

Amelia could hear Dion typing furiously in the background.

A few seconds later, he said, "Tell Catherine she can sign back into the system. I've made it obvious that it's under my jurisdiction."

"You didn't need to do that."

"I did it for Catherine." Dion ended the call.

Amelia put down her phone and nodded to her partner. "You still have access, but wait until the shift's over."

Perhaps now they could concentrate on the matter at hand.

Amelia pointed at the screen. "Do me a favour. Do a complete trawl of the location and count up the women."

Catherine did as she was asked. "I make it nineteen."

"There were twenty-two yesterday."

Catherine opened the day log. "It doesn't say here that any of them left."

140

There'd been no one on surveillance duty yesterday or last night. The priority had been meetings to prepare for full lockdown and everyone had been called off their ops to comply.

"I've emailed Pat but I doubt if there'll be any change in terms of process."

"Then what do you suggest?"

"I want to get a closer look."

Of course, Catherine could talk her out of this, but considering that she'd supported her over the Aleesha problem, it was unlikely that Catherine wouldn't support her colleague now.

"Let me get the gear together."

They had torches, both low- and high-powered, cameras that could be used through the smallest of cracks in masonry or brick, and armoured vests. That would have to do. They weren't preparing for a raid, just a quick recce and back.

By the time they reached the factory, they were using the low-powered torches pointed low to the ground. The last time they'd come this way, they'd found a gap in the fence in front of the warehouse close to the side of the canal. There was no towpath on that side. One slip and you were in. Amelia moved first, one step at a time, moving crablike against the bricks. She stopped when she found a suitably poor piece of mortar that was far enough away from the original cameras to give an alternative view.

Catherine followed and placed one hand on Amelia's back to steady her as she bored a hole and threaded the camera through it. They didn't have the lookouts they'd had previously, so Catherine kept her eyes firmly on the metal staircase at the side of the building. If they were caught now, then they might as well give up altogether.

The view through the small camera was far clearer. It picked up the worry lines on the women's faces. They all seemed to be sweating. Many were coughing into tissues. Amelia spotted Julie hunched up on the floor, wincing with every hacking cough. The gangmasters kept their distance. They had the luxury of keeping to the two-metre rule but even they looked worried.

Amelia spotted Cheun. He was standing at the door, speaking animatedly into his phone. Amelia tried to lipread what he was saying but it soon became clear that he was speaking Chinese.

It was four o'clock in the morning and, apart from a few women who seemed weaker than the others, everyone was awake. This wasn't good. Amelia withdrew the camera.

She whispered to her partner. "Something's happening."

Both women crept back through the gap in the fence. They didn't speak again until they were back on board the boat.

"My guess is that they'll dump the women — either leave them in the factory or take them somewhere else. We need back up either way."

Catherine nodded.

"Keep an eye out while I make a call."

In the half-hour it took to muster a team, there had been no movement. Amelia was beginning to worry that she'd called it wrong. Her instincts were usually strong, but maybe the men were prepared to just continue as they were and farm out the ill women to unsuspecting clients.

Catherine and Amelia waited in one of the cars, like everyone else. The assigned team comprised three vehicles of NCA armed officers. They would wait to see if other members of the OCG arrived to remove the women, or if the existing gangmasters decided to abandon them. If Cheun left, then they would follow him to see if he led them to other members of the OCG.

Of course, they could just be sitting there until first light. If that was the case, the unit would leave and only Catherine, Sean and Amir would be left. Worse than that, Amelia would have to explain why they had wasted a considerable amount of money and time on her watch.

Another hour ticked by with nothing happening. The early morning dawn chorus had begun. Officers stared at their phones and then at Amelia. She bit her lip. It was her call. Pat had given her that, no doubt to push the blame onto her subordinate if it was a waste of time and resources.

They all heard it at the same time. People were descending the metal staircase. Amelia picked up the walkie talkie in her lap. "We're on. Proceed at a distance."

Three men, including Cheun, walked across the street in front of them. Fortunately, they took no notice of the blacked-out windows of the unmarked parked cars. Cheun stopped beside an old Golf that flashed as he unlocked it. All three men entered the car – Cheun and another in the front, and one in the back.

The women had been abandoned. The Golf pulled away from the curb. Amelia rang Pat to initiate a rescue of the women. She had already relayed how ill they were and knew medical attention would be arranged for them, but now all eyes were on the getaway car and its occupants.

The three cars assigned for the purpose were joined by others as they snaked their way at a discreet distance through the centre of Birmingham. The Golf was in no hurry. There were few people about. Amelia spotted a newsagent putting his signs out on the rubbish-strewn pavement and a couple of nurses chatting at the bus stop. Other than that, the streets were unusually quiet even for this hour of the morning.

Reports continued of each turn the Golf made. The car Amelia travelled in hung back, as did the armed response unit. Instead, they let other officers in unmarked cars pursue and swap so as not to be spotted by the men in the Golf. The car drove on towards the A45 and out of town. Amelia knew this area of Birmingham well. When she didn't want to take the M6, she took this route from Coventry. Maybe that was where they were heading.

But then the Golf swerved and doubled back on itself. The lead chase car continued in the wrong direction but was backed up by another that was able to follow with a legal right turn across the carriageway. The rest of the entourage could follow suit. They were heading for Chinatown.

The Golf pulled up outside a Chinese supermarket, ignoring the double yellow lines. The three men brazenly exited the car and, instead of entering the supermarket, walked around to a side entrance that led to the restaurant above. Amelia told the team to hang back. There was no point storming the building to find the men sharing a dim sum. Yes, the restaurant should be shut due to lockdown, but they needed to catch them with other, higher-up members of the OCG to make the arrest worth it.

After five minutes, Amelia began to squirm in her seat. It was her call to make. "We'll go in as agreed."

The armed officers left their cars in unison along with two officers with an enforcer in case the backdoor was locked. Amelia followed behind.

They waited for a second at the door as one of the officers checked to see if it was locked. It was not. Amelia's pulse quickened. This wasn't right. The lead officers put down the enforcer and left it next to the door. Armed officers climbed the steps in formation. Any small sound would alert the men inside.

It took seconds to reach the restaurant. "Get down on the ground! Hands behind your head!" Amelia heard them before she reached the top of the stairs.

The three men from the car, plus a fourth wearing a white apron, lay face down on the floor with weapons trained on them. Three bowls of noodles sat steaming on the table.

Amelia nodded to one of the officers and each man was handcuffed and led out of the room. Amelia hit a table with a fist. *Fuck!* This wasn't how it was meant to end.

Chapter 19
Missing Women

Amelia expected to see a line of ambulances back at the factory, but there were none when she pulled up. She rang Catherine's number. She'd left her here to organise the evacuation. Amelia should have been at the local nick to interview Cheun and the others, but she needed to be sure the women were safe first.

Catherine didn't answer her phone. Amelia decided to check the building, believing her partner was at the hospital without a signal. She could not have been more wrong. The women were all still in the factory. Catherine was attempting to administer aid on her own as no other police or medical officers had arrived.

"What the fuck?"

Catherine stood up. "There are no free ambulances."

"It's been at least two hours!" Amelia scanned the scene… so many sick women. She quickly counted. Twelve, even fewer than before. "Where are the others?"

Catherine stared at her feet. "They ran off. I called it in..."

"So officers are out looking for them?"

Catherine shrugged.

This was a disaster.

"It's not your fault, it's mine. I should have been sure that the scene was contained before leaving to chase the perps."

But she had informed the local station and requested medical attention. This was crazy!

Amelia's phone vibrated in her pocket. She reached for it. Pat's name lit up the screen.

"Boss?"

"Where the hell are you?"

"I'm at the warehouse. We've got no support here." Amelia scanned the room. Where was Julie?

"You're supposed to be interviewing."

"This is our priority. Some of the women are missing and they're getting no medical attention. Where the fuck are the ambulances?" Julie was ill. She could be a risk to the wider population.

"There probably aren't any free. It's hell out there."

"Some of the missing women are ill, too. We need bodies to search for them."

"I'll see what I can do. Leave Catherine with them."

Amelia cut the call before she could say no. She turned to her partner. "I'm sure there'll be ambulances here soon. Can you triage?"

At least that would enable them to send the paramedics to the neediest first. Catherine walked the room, numbering and assessing each woman as she went.

Amelia searched for one who appeared to be least sick. She spotted one sitting on her own, studiously ignoring the others. When Amelia got closer to her, she realised it was the supervisor from the nail bar. The woman stared at her as she approached and then waved her arms around.

"No English," she hissed.

"Don't give me that bollocks. We've met before." Amelia waved her fingernails at her, though no one could now suspect that they'd ever been manicured. "You're going to help me

147

out here." The woman still wouldn't look her in the eye. "Where are the other women? What happened after the men left?"

The woman just shrugged and still refused to make eye contact.

"Fine. Then I'll arrest you as a gangmaster." Amelia reached for her cuffs.

The woman flapped her arms around. "Okay, okay."

"What's your name?"

"Linh Dan Cam."

Now Amelia could see her face, she realised that this woman was much younger than the matriarch she encountered before.

"What shall I call you?"

"Cam. It means mountain sunset, not that I'm ever likely to see one of those again."

"Thank you, Cam." Amelia paused. "We need your help. Where are the others? They're ill and they need medical help."

Cam shrugged. "They left as soon as the men did. I told them they'd be better off here but they didn't listen."

"Which way did they go?" They couldn't get far, sick as they were.

"I followed them out to the stairs. I tried to plead with them."

Amelia could imagine what that looked like. They were used to being bossed around by this woman. Maybe they realised they didn't have to listen to her anymore. "Which way, Cam?"

"Towards the nail bar. It's the only area they know, I guess."

"Thanks."

The door opened then. The first set of paramedics arrived, followed by a couple of police officers. Amelia spent the next ten minutes explaining to the officers where they should start their search. Catherine had done a great job of triaging, and within an hour they had a list of women who needed hospital treatment and the first few had been transported to the local hospital.

Amelia needed somewhere to take those who didn't need treatment. They still needed to be isolated. She bit her tongue and called her boss.

"So you've decided to get back in touch?"

"We need somewhere for those women who aren't ill enough to go to hospital to stay."

"You're not even supposed to be there." Pat sighed, "What about Poppy's?"

Amelia paused. Could she burden her friend with this? "Yeah, I'll ask Siobhan."

Siobhan had miraculously found room for the five women who did not need hospital treatment. Apart from Cam, they were all showing signs of the virus. By the time Amelia arrived at the refuge, Siobhan and her partner, Ellie, had moved some beds downstairs into the basement, cleaned the downstairs toilet facilities and provided a makeshift kitchen that only this group of women would use.

Siobhan smiled at Amelia. "Best we could do at short notice."

Amelia could have hugged her friend but, considering that she hadn't even worn a mask in the warehouse, that wasn't going to happen anytime soon. She could put herself at risk, but not others. "Thanks, Shiv. Have you got PPE?"

Siobhan held up a paper mask. "This, you mean?"

"Haven't the bloody council given you proper masks and aprons and shit?" Amelia fumed.

"This is it. A small box of masks."

Amelia glanced at her watch. It was 3:00 am. First thing in the morning, she would raid the council supplies depot and help herself to PPE for the refuge, but they'd have to make do for now. She helped Siobhan get the women settled.

At 5:00 am, Amelia left the refuge, planning to go home and at least get a few hours' sleep. Instead, she found herself driving to Michal's. She took the keys out of the ignition and stared at his door for a few minutes.

"Fuck it," she muttered.

If Michal was surprised to see her on his doorstep in the middle of the night during a lockdown, he didn't show it. In fact, he looked bemused. "I guess you'd better come in before anyone notices you and calls the police."

Amelia melted in his arms. This was all she needed.

The next morning, Amelia was woken up by loud chatter coming from the direction of Michal's kitchen. It sounded like he was hosting a party. She glanced at the clock on the bedside table — 8.10 am — groaned, and pulled the duvet over her head.

Michal entered the bedroom a few minutes later holding a tray. "Coffee and a cooked breakfast. Thought you might need it as you said that you have to be out early."

Amelia forced herself to sit up. "Thanks."

Michal passed her the tray and sat down on the edge of the bed. "As you probably noticed, I'm not on my own here. Half the family have isolated with me."

Amelia should have expected that. There was no way the rest of the clan would have let Michal spend lockdown on his own and the house was big enough for a few extras.

"I shouldn't have come."

'No, you shouldn't. But I'm glad you did... I'll take the rap." Michal held up his hands in a gesture of surrender.

"It won't happen again."

Michal smiled. "Don't promise that."

Amelia realised at that point that she hadn't contacted her own family. They were used to her not being home but, still, they'd probably be worried. She finished the toast and picked up her phone. There was already a missed call from Jola and one from Pat that she ignored.

Jola answered on the second ring. "Where are you?"

Amelia lied "Working. Everything okay?"

"No... it's not. It's your mum, Amelia. They've taken her in... her breathing's not good."

Michal took her other hand. "Which hospital, Jola?"

"Walsgrave, I think." Amelia could hear Jola sob. "But you can't go there. None of us can. It's not allowed."

Amelia had already got out of bed and started searching for her clothes.

Jola continued. "The girls —"
"Jola, I'll be there soon. But I'm going to

the hospital first."

Michal offered to drive, but Amelia was having none of it. Her badge would get her past the door.

A and E had been closed off with a sign directing visitors back to the main hospital entrance. There was a line of ambulances waiting to offload their patients. Amelia hoped to God that her mother wasn't in one of those.

The main entrance was partially shut, forcing everyone towards a makeshift reception desk. Amelia took out her badge and showed it to the receptionist. She didn't look impressed.

Amelia finally muttered, "My mother's been brought in."

The young receptionist sighed, "You can't be here."

"I just want to know that she's okay."

The receptionist repeated her monologue. "Don't worry. A member of her medical team will call you with updates."

"But they didn't even tell me that she's here!" Amelia rarely shouted at medical staff. They were more important than even fellow officers in her book. "Can you at least make sure they've got my number?"

The receptionist scrolled through something on her tablet. "Name of patient?"

"Jane Henson."

"Your details?"

Amelia rattled off her name and phone number.

"You'll have to leave now. Someone will be in touch soon."

For the first time, Amelia realised that this pandemic was serious. Deadly serious.

When she arrived home, she was greeted by two tearful children and their tearful nanny. She admonished herself for being such a shit mum that, instead of spending time with her family, she'd spent the last hours with strangers and her part-time boyfriend. It was no use lying to herself that she'd make it up to them, either.

At least Callum seemed oblivious. He just sat playing with his dinosaur whilst watching an episode of Peppa Pig.

They all sat down in the living room. Amelia was the first to speak. "What happened?"

"I knew something was wrong," Jola wailed. "She wasn't hungry, and she looked really hot and sweaty. She coughed and coughed but blamed it on the pollen."

Becky put her hand on Jola's arm. "It's not your fault, Jola."

"She got worse very quickly, so I called an ambulance."

Amelia's phone rang and everyone froze.

It was Pat, not the hospital. Amelia explained what had happened, which stalled her boss's rebukes.

As soon as Amelia cut the call, her phone rang again.

"Hi. I'm the sister on your mother's ward."

"Can I put you on speaker? The whole family's here."

There was a slight pause. "Yes, of course. It's just a quick update. Can I just confirm that I'm speaking to the daughter of Jane Henson?"

"That's right." Caitlyn had snuggled up to her on the sofa and Amelia put her arm around her.

"Your mother's comfortable. She's on the highest level of oxygen at the moment. I'm afraid we'll probably have to move her to ITU if she doesn't improve in the next couple of hours."

"Can I... can I speak to her?"

"If we do need to intubate, then we'll ring you so you can speak to her — unless, of course, we have to do that as an emergency... I'm sorry it's not better news."

Amelia was grateful for her frankness. As soon as she ended the call, she reached out to her daughters and pulled them close. Kissing their heads in turn, she whispered, "It'll be okay."

It seemed so unfair. It had barely been a few years since her mother's stroke. Why were they going through all this again as a family?

Caitlyn fell asleep in her mother's lap. Becky kept herself busy making teas and coffees, the silence only punctuated by texts and messages from friends and family. The television had been turned off at some point and Callum was running around poking everyone with his favourite toys. Fed up that no one was joining in his game, he eventually gave up and sat down to make towers with bricks.

Becky offered to make sandwiches for lunch. Amelia glanced at her phone. How could it be midday already? "I've got to work."

She tried to stand, cradling Caitlyn's head so she could place it on the sofa without disturbing her, but the girl stirred as soon as her mother moved.

"Sorry," Amelia muttered.

Caitlyn sat up, disorientated. She rubbed her face and it didn't take her long to realise that the situation remained as grave as when she had fallen asleep.

Jola pulled her into a hug. "Do you want something to eat, my angel?"

Caitlyn nodded and the two of them went to join Becky in the kitchen. Callum continued to play, oblivious of his mum's presence. It didn't take long for Amelia to settle on the sofa with her laptop. Catching up with her emails, it was clear that they'd survived the morning without her. Cheun and the other men from the warehouse had been interviewed and their "No comments" recorded. That was no surprise.

Catherine had been dispatched to Poppy's Place to interview the women who arrived there last night. It would be a few hours before any reports would be uploaded to Sharepoint. There was nothing for Amelia to do, other than wait for news.

Chapter 20
Kill Order

The Undertaker had new orders. Unexpected orders. His usual role was to get rid of the bodies but, this time, he'd been asked to search for live women, kill them by any preferred means, then bury them.

He relished the idea of being the hunter. He had the photos of the missing women in front of him to memorise. All were Southeast Asian and were likely to be living rough in the city centre. He just had to find them and slaughter them.

That morning, the city council had announced a clean-up of the city's homeless. All those still sleeping rough would be offered hostel accommodation during the pandemic. He had to act quickly. If they found their way into a shelter, they could end up anywhere in the city.

So he volunteered for one of the homeless charities, offering his services with his van. The group jumped at his offer. He would transport hot meals and leaflets as they roamed the city streets that evening.

Within an hour, he found a young Vietnamese woman hunched in a doorway. He handed her a mug of soup and smiled. She didn't smile back. "Been on the streets long?"

She sucked up the soup between toothless gums. "What's it to you?"

"Nowt."

He thrust a leaflet in her hand and walked off. She was of no interest to him.

Chapter 21
Sighting

Amelia spent the afternoon playing on the floor with Callum, making towers and racing his car collection. This went some way to explaining all the marks on the skirting board in the living room, which had remained a mystery to her up until now. Caitlyn helped by building garages and extravagant ramps out of Lego for the cars to slide down.

The hours passed, waiting for a call from the hospital that didn't come.

This could have been good — no call meant no change, or bad because the staff were too busy trying to save her mum to call and update. Amelia hoped it was the former and dreaded the latter.

Becky took on the role of comforter. She'd moved on from simply making teas and coffees and was now scouring recipe books for an evening meal. Amelia knew that none of this was normal. Her daughters' brave faces were hiding their fear and anxiety. They needed her to step up and support them with reassurance that their nan would be fine despite everyone knowing that this might not be the case. Amelia couldn't lie to them, so said nothing. She planned to work during the night and said nothing about that, either.

Finally, after they'd eaten Becky's excellent attempt at Hunter's Chicken, Amelia's phone lit up with the hospital's number.

It was the same ward sister as earlier. Amelia put her on speakerphone. "Hi. I just wanted to let you know that your mother is still comfortable. She's on maximum oxygen and is holding her own. Our concern is that she's tiring, and we'll ring you if we need to move her to intensive care.'

"Can we speak to her?" Becky asked as no one else had the words.

"I'll see if one of the nurses is free. Then I suggest you ring her phone. You could even use FaceTime or Skype if you have it. But it must be a short call — just a hello, really."

Amelia had no clue what phone her mother had or if she'd even taken it with her.

Jola stepped in. "I put her phone in her bag. It has Skype on it. She's used it with her knitting friends."

"Great. I'll ask the nurse to text you when she's able." The ward sister, Priya Prakash, then cut the call.

No one spoke for a minute or two. Then Jola said, "It's good that they keep in touch."

Becky wiped away a tear with her sleeve. "I'd rather be there with her."

"Of course." Jola looked ready to bolt back upstairs to her room. She wasn't coping well, which surprised Amelia as she usually was the first to step up in a crisis.

Caitlyn rubbed her eyes. "Can I stay up?"

There was no reason to get up early. It wasn't like she had school in the morning. She could complete the workbook they'd sent home with her on the last school day at any time.

"Sure," Amelia muttered. "Find a film or something we can all watch, and I'll put Callum to bed."

This lasted about half an hour. The film they chose wasn't bad. It was a British comedy with a good cast, which, on any other day, may have held their attention. But Caitlyn nodded off halfway through, Amelia had taken out her laptop and Becky had decided to read a textbook for her physics assignment. The drone of the television continued as background news.

More reports, which Amelia prioritised, had been shared. They'd found signs that the missing women had been at the nail bar during the day. The shutters were open and a vigilant neighbour had complained that they thought it might be open for business. Lockdown might actually make it easier to trace the women as there were so few people about and so many businesses were closed in the city centre. Last week, it had been like a ghost town.

The nail bar had been visited by local detectives, who only found sandwich and crisp wrappers. Amelia wondered if the runaways would try and go back that evening. She made a note to contact Sean. She could head over to the nail bar with him as soon as she'd spoken to her mum, if allowed.

The next reports were filed by Catherine, who had completed her interviews with the women at Poppy's. They made grim reading. Their stories were now so familiar to Amelia. They had been conned into believing they were coming to a new, exciting life in England, only to realise that they were to be prostituted to pay for their passage.

Sex trafficking occurred across the country from city to city and into the country. So little was done to protect these women and bring the perpetrators to justice that it enraged Amelia to the core. Maybe when this current crisis was over, the politicians would finally begin to believe these women, but Amelia doubted they would ever be top of anyone's agenda.

Lockdown made little difference. They would still find ways to provide for the needs of men who would pay for their services. Some of these might go online, but they were already getting reports of women disguised as fast-food delivery workers being sent to houses to deliver sexual services instead. Worse, some women had been "sold" for the duration of lockdown for a monthly fee so that they could be repeatedly raped by their captors. The transactions were picked up on the dark web by intelligence officers.

After the call with her mother that evening, Amelia rang Pat to check if she was still permitted to work. Ironically, she hadn't seen her mother in the last three days and, since no one else in the household showed any symptoms, her boss couldn't force her to self-isolate.

The phone call had been one of Amelia's worst five minutes. Her mother looked frail and vulnerable as she gasped for breath. She'd tried to smile whilst the girls spoke of their wishes for her to get well quickly and return home as soon as possible, but Amelia only saw pain. She shipped the girls off to bed as soon as the call was complete.

Amelia couldn't sit at home worrying a moment longer. Work was vital. Jola nodded when she told her that she was heading out to work. If Jola felt that this was inappropriate, she kept it to herself. She just sighed and said she'd keep an eye on the girls during the night as it was unlikely that she'd sleep.

Amelia drove to the nail bar to meet Sean. He was waiting outside for her, having obtained the keys from the landlord so that they wouldn't have to break down the door for a second time that day. He dangled them in front of Amelia.

"Do you want to do the honours?"

"Wait a second." Amelia didn't want to barge in on the women even if there was just a small chance they were there. They could bolt and then they'd be back to square one. She opened the letterbox slowly and peered in, then turned her head slightly to listen for any sounds of movement.

Assured that there was no one inside, she put the key in the lock and turned it. The door stuck a little, so she had to shove it open with her shoulder. Still no sound came from inside.

Amelia switched on the light. The local officers had been correct. There were signs of recent occupancy: a damp towel hanging on the back of a chair and empty packets of food on the table, just as they'd described in their report. They hadn't said if the women had broken in that morning or if the door was already damaged. Maybe they had a key and planned to return after dark. It would make sense.

The window wasn't shuttered as some of the local shops were. The blinds were thin, but it would be possible to get away with occupying the premises if they kept the lights off. Surely that was better than sleeping on the streets.

The nail bar was a small space with only a couple of seats for waiting customers, a counter at the front and six stations for the girls to work at. Their boss, Cam, used the shop counter as a reception desk and there was just enough space for her to walk between the stations to supervise the women's work and keep order.

If the women were planning to sleep here, then there wasn't much space for them to even lie down, but there was running water and a small toilet at the back. That was a luxury compared to the warehouse. If Amelia was in their shoes, she'd be back tonight.

Sean sat at the counter and Amelia sat on one of the customers' chairs. They both waited in silence, having decided to stake out the place for at least tonight.

A half-hour later, they heard some rustling at the back of the salon. Surely no one was attempting to climb in through the bathroom window? It was tiny. Amelia signalled for Sean to move towards the bathroom while she tiptoed towards the blinds. If one of the girls was getting in through the window, then she expected the others would be waiting to be let in through the front door. She peered through a gap but couldn't see anyone. Sean, meanwhile, was close to the bathroom door when they both distinctly heard another shuffling. Amelia motioned to Sean to open the door. He took his time. A black object shot across the floor as soon as he'd opened the door an inch. It was a rat! A bloody big rat! Amelia bit her tongue to stop herself from screaming. The rat disappeared under a cabinet containing boxes of nail polish.

"For fuck's sake…" Amelia could have left there and then.

Sean just laughed. "Got me going there for a bit."

As Amelia waited for her heart rate to calm down, she kept her eyes firmly on the cabinet. Hopefully, the rat had found a hole in the wall and wasn't coming back anytime soon.

The rest of the night passed without incident. No women. No more rats. She could have been at home but every corner searched was one less place to look.

Amelia spent most of the time in her own head. By morning, she'd convinced herself that she was responsible for her mother's illness — that she'd picked up an asymptomatic illness from work and brought it home to infect her, and that she was also a dreadful mother for abandoning her kids last night and going to work. Not only that, but the reason these women were now ill and on the streets was her fault, as she had failed to argue strongly enough on their behalf for the operation to be halted days ago and for them to receive medical attention. She didn't even spot that Sean seemed perfectly content with their role in the job. In fact, he seemed to think that they were going above and beyond. He mentioned a number of times during the night that they should have left this type of surveillance to junior officers.

Amelia didn't want to return home, so instead of going straight there, she took a detour to Poppy's Place. Ellie didn't seem at all surprised when she turned up at the front gate just after dawn. She let Amelia in and left her in the kitchen while she went to wake Siobhan. Amelia wondered if the two women were sleeping separately while Siobhan settled the new girls in. It made sense. Why risk them both catching the virus?

Siobhan entered the kitchen a few minutes later in full PPE. She took off her face shield and apron and sat down opposite Amelia at the large kitchen table. She kept her face mask on. She looked exhausted.

"Have you been up all night?" Amelia stated the obvious.

Her friend appeared to smile. "Yeah. A couple of them aren't well at all. I nearly called an ambulance but they're sleeping now."

"I can contact the hospital if you think they should be there."

Siobhan shrugged. "Shall I make coffee? Looks like we both need it."

"Thanks." Amelia thought that maybe she looked as bad as Siobhan did.

Siobhan went to the kitchen counter and flipped the switch to boil the kettle. She took two plain blue mugs out of a cabinet and placed them on the counter. "How's your mum?"

Amelia wondered for a moment how she knew, then quickly guessed that Carol had probably told her. She'd spoken to Carol briefly yesterday when she was at the end of her tether. The first thing Carol would have done was to ring Siobhan. They were like the three witches in Macbeth, the number of times they'd come together in mutual support.

"Hanging in there."

The kettle boiled and Siobhan finished making the coffee. Neither spoke until they'd had their first sips of the hot, restorative drink. Then Amelia said, "Thanks. For everything, I mean. You didn't need to take them in."

"Where else would they go?"

"But it puts the other women at risk." Amelia gestured towards the ceiling, knowing that the upper floors were full of other women that Siobhan had rescued. "I'm just surprised you said yes."

"We can keep them separate from the others in the basement. It's not luxurious, but it's better than where they've been living till now, so they tell me."

Amelia didn't like to tell her friend that she'd always found her cellar to be creepy… full of ghosts. But Siobhan knew that, knowing the house's history as a children's home run by paedophiles.

Their conversation was interrupted by the first risers of the day. Amelia recognised Leanne who, as a sex worker with a violent pimp, was a regular at Poppy's.

Siobhan immediately put back on her PPE. "Better go," she said. She disappeared downstairs before Leanne even came close to within two metres of her.

Amelia followed Siobhan to the basement door. "You'll need to be protected if you're coming down here." Siobhan pointed to the side room that Ellie used as her office.

In the office, Amelia found a small pile of PPE. She picked up a mask, face shield and gloves and made her way back to the basement door, putting them on as she went.

She caught up with Siobhan just as she was entering the makeshift bedroom. Four women lay on their beds. One, Cam, sat on a chair next to the youngest woman. She was holding a damp cloth to the girl's head. She didn't look up when the two women entered.

"How is she?"

Now Cam turned around. Gone was the aggression that she normally displayed. Now she could be the ill woman's parent. "A little better. Her temperature's breaking."

"Good," Siobhan said. "You remember Amelia?"

Cam grinned. "How could I forget?"

"We haven't found the others yet." Maybe one of these women would have an idea where the runaways would hide.

"I thought they might go to the nail bar." Cam continued to mop the girl's brow.

"They did, but they're not there now. I think they were frightened they'd be caught there."

"They'll be scared of being deported."

"They'd be better off."

Cam turned and stared at Amelia, her worry lines reappearing as she spoke. "Then they'd have the shame of explaining to their families what they've done while they were here."

"It's not their fault."

"We know that."

If they were deported, they might be back to living in poverty, but at least they would be safe. *Who was she trying to kid?* Amelia knew they wouldn't be safe in Vietnam. The Triads would search out their families and still demand payment in kind. Caught between a rock and a hard place, staying on the run might be their better option. They might never be found.

"We have the gangmasters that kept you, Cheun and the others." Might as well see what she knows, Amelia reasoned.

"Cheun is small. No one gives a fuck about him. He just kept us in line." Cam made a twirling motion by her head to imply that he was stupid.

"Did you meet any of the others?"

"Heard them talking sometimes. They'd meet outside the warehouse very late at night to pick up the money we'd made. Then they'd threaten Cheun and the others to keep their mouths firmly shut and keep us all quiet. We were just cash cows to them."

The girl that Cam was looking after moaned and opened her eyes. "Hey, little one. Want some water?" Cam poured her a glass. "Feeling better?"

It was time to leave. Amelia had a better picture of the dynamics in the factory. Cam cared about the girls in her own way, which was why she was harsh with them. She didn't want to risk their lives by allowing them to get cocky. Keeping them docile kept them all safe.

When Amelia got to her car, she did a quick sweep of her emails. One caught her attention. A group of volunteers for a homeless charity had spotted a small group of Southeast Asian women sleeping under the railway arches near New Street. There was no point heading over there now as they wouldn't stay there while it was light. She forwarded the report to Catherine and asked her to meet her there later tonight. Then she headed home.

Her kids were all in the kitchen eating breakfast. It was a late start for them. Usually, the girls would be in school by now. Everyone looked pale and drained. No one asked Amelia where she'd been. It was understood that she'd been at work, expected even.

Jola looked up and simply said, "Any news?"

Amelia shook her head. She reached for a cereal dish. She should at least eat something.

The doorbell rang. Amelia went to answer it. A delivery driver wearing a mask was standing behind a huge pile of boxes. He took a photo and muttered, "Thanks."

"What's all this?" Amelia said to no one in particular.

Jola had come to see. "Caitlyn, it's your workout stuff."

"What?"

Jola had already picked up the first box. "We'll put it in the back garden for now." She started to walk it through the house.

Amelia picked up a box and followed her. Caitlyn had joined the procession carrying one of the smaller boxes. It took them all a few trips to move the entire delivery from the front door to the garden.

"Anyone wish to explain?" asked Amelia, panting.

"It's my boxing stuff."

Amelia stared at Caitlyn, hoping she'd elaborate.

Jola explained, "Michal thought it would be a good idea for Caitlyn to continue her training at home, so we bought this."

"On my credit card, no doubt." Not that it was an issue. The issue was that, as usual, Michal hadn't even thought to mention it to her.

"Yeah. We didn't think you'd mind." Jola had already started opening the boxes.

At least all this was a distraction. Caitlyn was jumping up and down as each box was opened.

"Looks like we need to assemble these. Maybe we should skype Michal later for help?"

Caitlyn stopped jumping. Amelia could

almost taste her disappointment.

"I'll sort it."

Of course, what Amelia should have done is leave them to it and get some sleep. Instead, she spent the next three hours getting more and more grumpy and short-tempered as she attempted to assemble the gear. In the end, she had to admit defeat and call Michal. After she'd finished calling him all the names under the sun, he explained how each part should look once completed. She undid a few bolts, put them back in the right order, and Caitlyn finally had her own mini boxing gym. Amelia left her in the garden punching a speedball.

Amelia got a little sleep, half expecting a call from the hospital, but none came. It was only when she'd met up with Catherine in the centre of Birmingham that it crossed her mind that she could be denying her children the last chance of speaking to their nan before they put her in an induced coma, should the need arise. It was an awful thought, but Amelia knew that if the medics had to make a quick decision, they weren't going to wait for her to race home to get everyone in the room to speak to her.

Catherine appeared to be fighting her own demons, too. Amelia spoke to her twice before getting her colleague's attention. "I suggest we try to speak to the volunteers first. They start their shifts about now from St Michael's Church."

It was just a short walk away. The first person they saw was a small, balding man loading food parcels into his truck. Amelia introduced herself and said, "I'm looking for Stephen Standege."

The man stopped what he was doing and smiled. "Why do you need him?"

"Is he here?"

The man stuck his hands in his pocket and didn't speak for a moment.

"Well?"

"He's inside talking to the vicar." Then he turned back to the van and pushed a tray further in.

Catherine and Amelia entered the church and nearly bumped into a man taking off his face mask as he left.

"Stephen?" Amelia asked.

"Yes," he spluttered.

Amelia nearly put her hand out to shake. "We've come about the Vietnamese women. Can we go back inside?"

"Sure." Stephen was even taller than Amelia but had a natural stoop. If Amelia had to guess, then she'd put money on him not being keen to talk to the police.

The church was far less ornate on the inside than Amelia imagined. There were no large religious statues or the usual silver ornaments that you might expect. The lectern stood on a tabletop rather than a pedestal. Maybe this was the price of having a church slap bang in the middle of a city. Everything of value had to be locked away, or maybe it was simply because they weren't allowed to open the doors for services.

Stephen sat down in one of the pews at the back of the church, shuffling along to allow for space between them. Amelia sat at the end and rummaged in her bag for a notepad.

"I've not seen any new women, to be honest. On the streets, I mean." Stephen sat with his hands jammed together between his thighs.

"And if you did, you'd tell us." It was framed as more of an order than a question.

"Yes, of course." He looked away towards the vicar, who was hovering in the background.

Amelia wasn't convinced. "These women could well need urgent medical attention. They may have contracted the coronavirus and in their weakened state —"

"I do understand, officer."

"They've been kept in the most appalling conditions for the past few months."

"You need to understand that everyone I deal with lives rough. They hardly live in luxury."

"Then you'll understand why we're worried."

Stephen shrugged.

"Would you at least let the other volunteers know that we're looking for a group of South-East Asian women? I'd urge you not to approach them but to let us know immediately where they've been spotted."

"I'll do that."

Amelia stood, knowing that she was going to have to do some of the legwork herself. Catherine had spoken to a few of the volunteers by the time she got outside.

"Anyone seen anything?"

Catherine nodded. Earlier this evening, one of the volunteers spotted a group of women under a canal bridge near the Sea Life Centre. By the time he reached them, they'd upped and gone."

"We'll start there, then."

There were several canal bridges in the vicinity of the Sea Life Centre. It stood on the junction of the Birmingham and Fazeley and

the Birmingham Mainline Canals. Usually, at
ten in the evening, this area would be teeming
with life. The indoor arena and the convention
centres were nearby. There were also many pubs
and restaurants, including the one where
President Clinton had been filmed drinking on
the balcony many years ago.

"They're not likely to be at the exact
same spot as earlier, but it's worth checking
out places where they'd find some shelter."

Both women glanced around trying to suss
out possibilities. They both spoke at once,
suggesting the same area. The restaurants and
shops were likely to all be closed up. It made
sense that they'd be a good hideout. They
might even find some stored tins of food and
the owners were unlikely to be around much.

They struck lucky on the first stop. The
back door of Café Rouge was hanging on its
hinges. Rather than scare anyone inside,
Amelia shouted, "Hello?" into the back of the
restaurant.

She didn't expect an answer but at least
the occupants knew they were being visited.
The first room they entered was a staff area.
The doors of the staff lockers were wide open.
It was likely that the staff had emptied them
before leaving rather than risk them being
broken into. There were still a couple of
jackets hanging up on hooks along the wall.

Amelia would have expected to hear some
noise if the restaurant was occupied, but
there was silence, apart from some ominous,
intermittent scratching. The last thing Amelia
wanted to spot was another rat, but they at
least needed to check each room. If they
didn't find anything, then she would phone
through to the local police station so the

manager could be contacted to get the door
fixed.

Catherine opened a door. It led to a
half-empty storeroom. Any produce with a short
shelf life had been removed but there were
still some cans of drink and food on display.
The packets were open and empty cans littered
the floor. "Someone's been here, then. It
would take a pretty big rat to open those,"
Catherine observed.

She'd heard the noises, too then, Amelia
thought.

The main restaurant door was on the left
and the kitchen on the right. Amelia and
Catherine searched these and the toilets, but
there was no one around.

Catherine found some tissues on the floor
of the women's toilets. They didn't have to
handle them to notice they were speckled with
blood. Amelia called this in. Maybe the women
had been here after all.

Chapter 22
Stalker

The undertaker followed the two officers at a distance. He knew who they were looking for — the same prey as him, but he couldn't be the follower. He had to lead the hunt. He had to capture the women and kill them before they were discovered and placed somewhere out of his reach.

It made sense that they'd be near the canal. That was all they knew of the city. That and the footpath to the nail bar, but he'd checked that area already.

What surprised him was how easy it had been to find the other group of women, those not on the streets.

He sat in a lay-by the next morning less than a mile from Poppy's Place and planned his next steps.

Chapter 23
Priorities

The call came at nine the next morning. Amelia had slept lightly for an hour since her night shift, her mind and body on alert with the expectation of being disturbed.

"Hi, Amelia. It's Priya from the hospital. I'm afraid your mum's taken a turn for the worse. Her oxygen levels fell rapidly during the night and we had to move her to the ICU."

Amelia let that sink in for a moment. "Can I speak to her?"

"I'm so sorry, Amelia. We had to ventilate her. It happened so quickly that it would have been too risky to call you first."

Amelia choked, "What are her chances?"

"It's early days and you must understand that we're learning as we go and finding new treatments that can help. But I have to be honest with you, once a patient is on a ventilator, the chances of survival aren't great."

"Thank you for being honest. I appreciate that."

Amelia knew that she'd need to be just as honest with the others. There was always hope for recovery, but they needed to prepare for the worst.

Amelia took a shower and got dressed before delivering the news. Her children and Jola were sitting at the dining room table when she got downstairs. Jola had taken on the role of teacher and prepared lessons for them all, including Callum, who was matching blocks with the appropriate holes in a plastic box. They all looked up expectantly when Amelia sat down.

Jola motioned for the girls to close their books.

Amelia didn't know how to start. Becky started to cry before she'd said a word. She wiped her face on her sleeve as Amelia began. "It's not good news."

Caitlyn howled, "Is she dead?"

Amelia placed her hand on her youngest daughter's arm. "No. Not dead."

"But it's bad…" Becky stared at the table, not wanting to catch her mother's eye.

"She's been sedated. It's like a long sleep to help her to breathe better."

"Like a coma?" Becky asked.

"Yes, a coma. A long sleep. Then, hopefully, while she rests, her body can recover."

"Can we see her?" Caitlyn grabbed her mum's hand and held it tightly.

"No, not at the moment. No one's allowed to see her in case we catch it."

Caitlyn folded her arms. "I don't care if I catch it."

"Well, I do." Jola picked up Callum, who had picked up on the prevailing mood and started to grizzle.

No one spoke for the next few minutes. Callum played with Jola's necklace and everyone else was lost in their own thoughts.

It was Becky who broke the malaise. "This is all my fault."

Amelia looked up. "What?"

Becky stood up, tears streaming down her face. "I sneaked out to see Harry, so it's my fault she's dying." Then she ran off upstairs.

Amelia escaped to her office. She'd tried

to console her daughters, but they needed their own space, too. Becky wouldn't listen, convinced that the illicit trip to meet her boyfriend had caused her grandmother's illness. Amelia blamed herself for not being able to take their pain and fear away. She'd hoped to catch up on paperwork but became distracted by the daily statistics. The numbers of new infections, hospital admissions and deaths were all rising rapidly. Her mother was just one amongst many. Sixty per cent of those on ventilators died within a week. Amelia closed her laptop.

Catherine called just at the right time. She'd been told by the Somerset police that they'd had a sighting of her niece. "You don't need me for the next couple of days."

This was a statement, not a question, and took advantage of Amelia's good nature. Amelia couldn't think straight and understood the pull of family right now, rather than work. So many had lost or were concerned about vulnerable relatives. No one chose to be a key worker rather than on furlough. It had been foisted on them. But, of course, the police, NHS and teachers had always been frontline.

Amelia hadn't realised she'd drifted off to sleep at her desk until her dreams were disturbed by her shrieking ringtone. Siobhan's name lit up the screen.

Amelia answered with a mumbled, "Hello?"

It wasn't Shiv who spoke, but Ellie. "You've got to send police... now... someone's trying to break in."

No other words were needed. Amelia cut the call with Ellie and called her boss. She already had her coat on and her car keys in her hand by the time she'd explained that there was an emergency at Poppy's Place.

Amelia broke the speed limit on the short journey. Approaching the security gates of the refuge, she was shocked to see them wide open. Ellie was meticulous about keeping them shut. Amelia grabbed the steering wheel tighter as she sped down the gravel road.

A sea of blue lights illuminated the front drive. The local police had beaten her to it. Amelia could now breathe and went in search of her friends.

Ellie was giving a statement to a detective whose name escaped Amelia. Siobhan sat at the opposite end of the kitchen table cradling a coffee and still wearing a plastic apron and gloves.

"What the fuck happened?" Amelia asked her friend.

"Some idiot tried to break in over the wall." Siobhan ran her hand through her unruly curls. "Of course, he didn't expect us to be alarmed to the hilt."

The refuge had suffered its fair share over the years of angry pimps trying to storm the refuge looking for the women they lived off illicitly. A good chunk of money had been spent on an alarm and CCTV system. That was without the strength and tenacity of its security guard, Ellie. Did that woman ever sleep?

"Has he been caught?" Amelia expected the answer to be negative.

"Only on camera." Siobhan led Amelia to Ellie's office.

Along the back wall sat a bank of monitors, each covering the garden and various entrances to the site. Siobhan typed an instruction into Ellie's laptop and the middle monitor changed to show a grainy picture of a man placing a blanket over the razor wire on top of the wall, about a 100 metres away from the front gate. The man pulled himself up onto the top of the wall. He carried a large rucksack on his back. Amelia dreaded to think what was in it. Almost immediately, the area was lit up by security lightening. Startled, the figure jumped back down off the wall the way that he had come. Leaving the blanket, he ran towards the woods at the back of the house.

Someone coughed behind the two women. Amelia jumped and turned. The detective whose name she now remembered as Roberts or Robertson stood in front of her. "Any idea who he might be?"

Amelia was unsure whether he was asking Siobhan or her. Siobhan shrugged. Amelia said, "None. Could be a local pimp but, to be honest, if he was angry enough the lights wouldn't have stopped him." Ellie had rugby-tackled a fair number of them over the years. This guy was either easily put off or didn't want to get caught.

"Ellie says you've got a group of new girls in. Where are they from?"

Up until this point, Amelia would have considered him one of the good guys, the more enlightened ones who had completed the equality training and learned something from it. "The women are part of a group recently trafficked from South-East Asia. They've been forced to work as prostitutes and in a nail bar, but they were dumped after many of them contracted coronavirus."

"Does he look Chinese to you?" The DI nodded towards the screen.

Amelia wasn't sure if he was seeking agreement or making some kind of facetious comment. "I don't think the picture's clear enough to ascertain his race."

"Look, Amelia —"

"DI Barton."

"Well, if we're going down that route, you'd better start calling me DCI Roberts."

Since when had this idiot become a DCI? Siobhan had her head down, stifling a grin. Perhaps she knew what was coming.

Roberts couldn't let it go. "I know you NCA lot have to be all PC and that. And I'm not talking about one of our constables." He then had the temerity to wink. "But —"

Amelia took a step forward, invading his space. "If you mean how we seek to treat all women with respect, try to recognise our unconscious bias and are not inherently racist, then that would be the aim. Unfortunately, some people still need to work on that." Her voice rose as she spoke.

DCI Roberts' face turned beetroot red and Siobhan burst into uncontrollable laughter.

Before Roberts could say another word, Amelia pushed past him into the kitchen. No one looked in her direction except Ellie, who raised her eyebrows. Amelia ignored them all and grabbed herself a coffee from the flask that someone had set up on the sideboard. Siobhan arrived at her side shortly after.

"I enjoyed that," she whispered. "Oh, and you'll be pleased to know that the women downstairs are all improving. Cam's come down with it, but she's not too bad, either. How are the ones at the hospital?"

Amelia had received an email about them earlier. "All on the mend. I don't suppose —"

Siobhan sighed. "I just haven't got the room."

"We'll have to split them up, then, and see if anyone else can accommodate them." They might have to force them to. There weren't many hostels that would take in women still possibly infectious with a deadly virus.

"For fuck's sake!" Siobhan slammed down her mug. "If you can get me some beds, then I can fit them in."

Amelia moved to hug her friend then remembered the two-metre rule and backed off. "Thanks. You're an angel."

"And I'll need some more fucking PPE."

Amelia took her time driving home. She'd had to smarmy up to DCI Roberts in the end as she needed him to provide some surveillance for Poppy's Place. It had taken some doing. No one liked being shown up in front of junior officers, especially not by a junior officer.

Roberts had only turned up to the refuge break-in because he was already in the area. His sister had been taken ill and he'd faced the same as Amelia. Despite driving to the hospital, he hadn't been allowed in. It wasn't an excuse for him being ignorant, though, and Amelia didn't regret telling him that for one moment.

The house was dark when she arrived home. A meal had been left for her in the fridge. Amelia sat down at the table to eat it and suddenly started to sob. Each mouthful of food turned grainy and unchewable in her mouth. She forced herself to eat only because she couldn't afford to be ill. As soon as she finished, she went to the bathroom and washed her hands. She hadn't bothered all day. Great example she was! She couldn't even get that bit right.

Amelia had forgotten the 8:00 am Teams meeting. It was only when Will sent her a text saying WHERE THE FUCK ARE YOU? that she fired up her laptop.

When the call connected, she mumbled, "Sorry, bad internet connection." She was twenty minutes late. All the others on the call appeared to have already given Pat a brief overview of their current cases. Most of them seemed to be in their living rooms or even bedrooms. One or two had their cameras off. At least Amelia had a dedicated place to work at home. That was down to her husband's untimely death and her mother selling her house and moving in. It had left them enough money to build an extension.

Amelia suddenly realised that Pat had said her name but hadn't a clue in what context. Everyone on the screen seemed to be staring at her.

Pat said, "You need to unmute."

Unmute and say what?

Amelia found the right icon on the screen and asked, "Sorry, what was the question?"

Instead of everyone grinning at her for her obvious lack of attention, they all looked concerned, which worried Amelia more.

Eventually Will spoke. "She's probably too busy remembering how she tore Ben Roberts a new arse."

Amelia smiled. News travelled fast. She'd been expecting a bollocking, but it was obviously seen as an us-and-them battle.

Pat interjected, "Best not go there. Amelia, have you got an update on Operation

Caludon?"

Amelia kept it short and to the point. Unless the women were able to identify anyone else, or Cheun or one of the other gangmasters ratted on someone higher up the food chain, the operation was over. The other women still needed to be found, but that was more of a public health exercise. They would throw the book at those in custody if the CPS agreed to take it forward. There was plenty of evidence of human trafficking including sex trafficking.

But there was nowhere left to go. Maybe Catherine was right. It was then that she noticed that Catherine wasn't in the meeting. Amelia hoped she wouldn't be bollocked for that, too.

An hour later, Amelia was completing some paperwork when her email pinged. It was from DI Starley and was short and sweet. CAN YOU GIVE ME A RING ABOUT ALEESHA COLEMAN ASAP. DOM.

Great. Now it looked like Catherine was causing her more problems. Instead of picking up the phone, Amelia decided to pay him a visit. She texted him instead. WHERE ARE YOU? SHALL WE MEET?

It was a warm day, so Amelia was pleased Dominic had suggested the park. When she got there, she was surprised to see so many people around. This appeared to be the place to come for daily exercise. Everyone seemed to have suddenly become a dog walker, though most people were avoiding the paths and kept their distance from each other.

Dominic had said that he'd meet her at the cafe. It was boarded up, as she expected but, sitting on the wall in front of it was DI Starley, holding two flasks. He raised one as she approached. "Thought I'd keep the coffee separate. Don't want to be spreading germs."

Amelia sat down and opened her flask, gratefully taking a large gulp. She had to give him credit — Dom could make good coffee.

He smiled. "Where's your sidekick?"

"DS Brown?"

"Yeah."

Probably best to be honest. "Looking for her niece, I expect."

Dominic looked at the floor and then raised his head. She hadn't noticed before how strikingly blue his eyes were. She shuffled a little away from him, obviously too close if she could see that.

He seemed bemused. "Thought so. We had a sighting of Aleesha but she's gone to ground."

"Oh."

"We've found the two young kids who were with her, which is good —"

"They're okay?"

"Yeah. They're fine. They were used as drug mules. Aleesha sent them to drop off gear to a few addresses. Young kids outside in a pandemic is an okay thing, apparently."

Amelia hadn't noticed. It was only the lack of cars she'd been paying attention to.

She bit her lip. "I hope you don't think Catherine's hiding her?"

"Aleesha?" Dominic's eyebrows crinkled. "I hope not, for her sake."

"If I hear from her —"

"— You'll probably not tell me," he smiled.

Amelia took another gulp of coffee.

"Probably not."

"Look, I know you want to protect your partner but this isn't going away. Aleesha's in it up to her neck."

Amelia nodded. "I know. She's trafficked kids."

"And she's still a kid herself."

Situations like this were complicated. How much coercion was Aleesha experiencing? Was she a victim, too?

Neither of them spoke for a while. Then Dominic asked, "How's your mum?"

How did he know she was ill? "Not good."

"I heard from a mate that she's unwell. I guess everyone's worried. And knowing someone's really unwell with it... it makes you think."

Amelia glanced around the park. It could be a day like any other except that there were loads of kids out who should have been in school. But then she saw that the playground was taped off and all the children were with a parent. There wasn't a group of teenagers congregating in the shelter or tearing around on skateboards. There wasn't anyone sitting on the grass enjoying the sun.

Dominic stood. "Call me."

Amelia nodded. She attempted to pass him his flask.

"Keep it until next time."

Why did his words make her heart beat a little faster?

Chapter 24
Goodbyes

Amelia knew where to find Aleesha, or at least she had a good idea. She strode up to the house and rapped on the door, though not too hard. She didn't want the occupants to think it was the police.

The door was opened by a teenage girl with tight braids. She took one look at Amelia and took to her heels. Amelia had already checked out the back of the house. She sprinted across the front lawn, nearly tripping over the decorative wooden edging and ran to block the exit from the side alley. The fleeing girl careered into Amelia moments later, almost knocking Amelia over.

Amelia stood firm, arms outstretched to stop the escapee going any further. Catherine joined them as her niece tried to squirm her way out from under Amelia's long limbs.

Amelia stared at her partner. "I take it this is Aleesha."

Catherine grasped the flailing girl's right arm and she stopped struggling quite as hard. "Let's go back inside." Catherine kept her voice steady and calm.

"Good idea." Amelia followed them.

She'd have done the same, to be honest. If one of her girls was this deep in trouble, she'd have hidden them if necessary, but would have also known that she'd be caught out at some point. Catherine had three kids of her own. She had hoped, maybe, that one more wouldn't cause her neighbours much concern. If they did wonder who the new girl was and why she was staying there, they'd just assume that their neighbour, being a police officer, had a good reason. Maybe she was a relative whose own family couldn't support her? Or perhaps she was a child of another frontline worker who wanted to protect her? If Amelia hadn't known that her partner had some inkling where Aleesha was hiding out, it might have worked.

Catherine opened the back door and, for the first time, Amelia entered her partner's kitchen. It was as neat and spotless as Amelia's, but this would be Catherine's doing. Amelia didn't keep her house clean and tidy. Jola and her mother saw to all that.

Amelia sat down at the kitchen table with Aleesha as Catherine closed the door to the rest of the house. She obviously didn't want her daughters to hear what was to follow.

"I can't pretend this hasn't happened," Amelia said as her partner took a seat.

Catherine nodded. Aleesha looked ready to bolt. Her legs twitched as she fidgeted.

Amelia's phone rang before she could say anything else. It was the hospital.

"I need to take this."

Amelia said very little during the call. Catherine and Aleesha stared at her. They could have bolted, but neither moved.

Amelia ended the call with, "Thank you… for everything." Then she turned to Catherine. "Take her in. It's the only option."

Everyone knew what Amelia was about to say when she walked in through her own front door, just as Catherine had known without asking. Grief can't be hidden. It ravages.

She held her girls for ages in the hall until they had no strength left to weep. Jola held onto Callum, repeatedly kissing his head as he squirmed in her grip.

There were no words.

When her husband died, Amelia had collapsed and relied on her mother for everything. She couldn't remember what happened in those first hours or days. They were empty pages in her life. Now her mother was dead, what was she supposed to say or do?

Between bouts of sobbing, Jola took charge. She made pots of tea despite Amelia only ever drinking coffee, and plates of sandwiches that were left to curl on the dining room table.

Amelia held her girls close on the settee. No one wanted to move. The room grew steadily darker but no one reached to turn on the lamps.

The letterbox rattled and Amelia stirred, not sure who to expect and not sure how she'd handle anyone else's grief.

She opened the door to Michal, who swept her up. "Jola rang me. I'm so sorry."

It seemed Michal had experience in handling the bureaucracy of death. Over the next two days, he steered Amelia and kept her afloat during the tidal wave of grief.

At times, she felt immense guilt. Guilt for not being a good daughter or a good mum to her children. Guilt for not telling her mother that she'd forgiven her years ago for any failings and loved and appreciated her. Guilt for breaking the rules – allowing Michal into her home, not being careful enough about wearing PPE and two-metre distancing. Guilt over bringing this virus into their home. Guilt for not working when the missing women needed her. Waves and waves of guilt and grief.

Michal held her head above water with his

list of what needed to be done. Fortunately, they didn't have to wait. An old lady dying of this dreadful virus didn't cause a stir. There was no need for a post-mortem. She would just be one statistic among many as the number of hospital deaths continued to rise. The funeral numbers would have to be small, mostly just close family. Amelia left Jola with the task of working with her mother's knitting group to decide on their representative. It seemed that a number of them were ill, which made Amelia fleetingly wonder if that was the source… the area's own mini version of the Cheltenham races.

Cars, flowers, donations and a celebrant were all sorted ready for the following Tuesday. It kept Amelia busy. Each tick on Michal's list was a minor achievement while he coached Caitlyn, played with Callum and sat watching movies with the girls. And then, each evening and night, he held her.

Tuesday came too quickly. Michal was tasked with staying at home with Callum and Caitlyn. One minute Caitlyn wanted to attend, but not the next. Amelia understood. In the end, they let her decide on the day. The cars left in a procession of two. The few people on the streets stared as they drove past. Amelia guessed they were wondering how her mother had died. Could she be one of that ever-growing number? She didn't catch their eye, just stared out of the opposite car window.

The funeral celebrant, Lisa Dundas, met them at the crematorium. Warmth exuded from her despite the social distancing rules. Amelia had chosen her because of her compassion when leading a murdered woman's funeral. She'd woven a story of a beautiful young woman's life that rose above the tragedy of her death. Amelia wanted today to be a celebration of the tenacity and strength that her mother had shown — turning her own life around and saving Amelia's. She'd never said that to her mother in life; maybe she could atone in death.

Becky read a poem chosen by her grandmother — *Remember*, by Christina Rossetti. Amelia thought that she couldn't have chosen anything better; the words cut deep and true. Her brave daughter read with dignity and passion.

The service came to an end as the heavy curtains closed in front of the coffin. The few mourners filtered out slowly. Amelia waited with her arm around Becky's waist. She thanked Lisa and then stood in front of the dull, beige curtains. In her head, she said her final goodbye.

Amelia spotted Catherine as she exited the crematorium. She was standing away from the mourners and didn't motion to Amelia to join her. Amelia did the dutiful goodbyes and thanks. There were only a few other mourners besides Becky, Jola and herself. Her mother would have filled the place if they'd been permitted to.

Eventually, Amelia joined her partner. Becky and Jola headed for the car to wait.

Catherine rubbed her hands on her trousers before speaking. "I'm so sorry."

Amelia shrugged.

Catherine continued, "Aleesha's been remanded on bail. She's back at mine." She continued, "Fortunately, I didn't have to account for the lost time."

What did she want her to say? In the end,

Amelia settled for, "It's for the best."

Catherine nodded. "Sorry."

Amelia walked away. She needed to get home.

Amelia went back to work the day after the funeral. She decided to go into the office and give her family some breathing space. She was the only one there as she signed on to the morning's Teams meeting. Everyone else was at home on their laptop.

Pat looked surprised to see her. "Amelia! We didn't expect you back yet."

"Nice to know you've missed me." Amelia switched her camera on so they could all see that she was fine.

Catherine turned her camera off.

A few condolences and sympathetic comments were murmured, then they moved on to business. Amelia had found the time to think while not working. There were too many loose ends. So, when Pat suggested that they close the Operation Caludon investigation, Amelia sat forward in her chair. "We can't."

Pat sighed. "I don't think there's anything else to be gained."

"There's still a group of missing women —"

"It's not our jurisdiction now, more like Public Health's."

No one else spoke up for Amelia, not even Catherine. Sean and Amir weren't on the call. Pat had evidently ended their secondment.

"What about the missing group of men? Or the other gangmasters? Are we just letting them off the hook?"

Pat called on Will. "Do we have any further intelligence on the OCG? Anything from the women we found?"

Will took his time to unmute. "A few hazy descriptions of men who were held at the factory. Nothing substantial."

"Then I'm sorry, Amelia, we've reached a dead end." Pat wouldn't look her in the eye. "Finish off the paperwork including the national referral mechanism forms this week and I'll assign you and Catherine to a new case on Monday."

Just like that.

Amelia felt a complete failure. Cheun might do a bit of time, but the others? No one could state categorically that the women weren't at risk, even those in hospital or at Poppy's. No one had been found responsible for the break-in. Amelia slammed down the lid of her laptop and went in search of coffee. Even the milk in the fridge was sour.

Amelia knew where she could get good coffee and better company. Siobhan looked concerned when Amelia turned up in her kitchen.

"Did you want me to phone ahead?"

"No, of course not. Coffee?" Siobhan stood to fetch her a drink and then noticed the mug on the table. "Oh, I see you've helped yourself."

"I've come to see Cam." Amelia took a long gulp of the bitter brew and sighed.

"You're not working?!" Siobhan looked horrified.

Of course she was bloody working. What did everyone expect? That she'd stay at home and do the housework?

Then Siobhan smiled. "I thought you'd be staying home, playing happy families with

Michal."

It should come as no surprise that her friends had been gossiping behind her back. But it was probably best that this wasn't common knowledge. As a police officer, she should be following the COVID rules, not breaking them at every opportunity.

"He's just staying a few days. I needed him to look after Callum so we could attend the funeral." Amelia finished her coffee. She wanted to get down to business, not chat with her friend. "His family's not best pleased. They'd all left their homes and moved into his to keep him company."

Amelia imagined this game of musical chairs. She understood how Alicia and her cousins felt, but it had all been Michal's idea, really. Alicia and Siobhan were instrumental in getting Amelia and Michal together in the first place. Alicia was one of the agency's interpreters and Michal's niece. She'd set the two of them up with the encouragement of Siobhan as a way of "protecting" Amelia. And he had. He'd saved her life and she couldn't forget that.

Amelia glanced up at Siobhan. "He's been great, to be honest. Now, can I see Cam?"

Cam didn't look all that pleased to see Amelia. The other women had gone outside to sit in the sun. They were all nearly recovered, whereas Cam seemed to be at the sharp end of the virus. Every time she moved, her body tensed, wracked with coughs. For once, Amelia was pleased that she'd been given full PPE.

She sat down as far away from the bed as she could and said, "I need your help, Cam."

Cam tried to speak but started

spluttering again.

Amelia continued. "I know you know more than you're saying."

Cam looked lost; her dark eyes squeezed shut with each bout of coughing. She couldn't speak.

"The thing is, if you don't give us more, you'll either be deported or charged with human trafficking."

Cam reached for a glass of water and took a long gulp. "If I speak to you then I'm dead anyway."

"So you want to go back and put your family at risk?"

Cam turned to the wall. "I just wanna be left alone."

"That's not happening anytime soon." Amelia folded her arms.

Cam didn't speak for ages. The two women were at an impasse, waiting to see who was the most stubborn.

Not speaking for a while calmed Cam's cough. She finally turned around and faced Amelia. "So, I can stay in the UK if I give you something?"

Amelia unfolded her arms. "I can't promise you that."

Cam rolled back over. "No immunity. No leave to remain. No speak.'

"Fine." Amelia reached for her mobile and stood up, knowing this wasn't going to be an easy conversation with her boss.

Amelia waited in the kitchen at Poppy's Place for a return call from Pat. Instead of a call, she was surprised to find that DCI Carol Jamieson had been sent to Poppy's instead. Her friend greeted her without the customary hug and sat down at the table.

"I hear you've got one for me."

Amelia was pleased that Carol hadn't done the whole, "I'm so sorry… how are you?" routine. "For the PPU?"

"Yeah. Linh Dan Cam, my notes say."

So Pat had already contacted the Public Protection Unit? That was quick.

"Yeah. She's downstairs but she has COVID." Amelia wasn't sure what she'd do with that information since, in the absence of any testing, they were supposed to assume everyone had it.

"I've got PPE in the car. I'll grab it before I take her in."

Siobhan had been hovering. "You can have some of our meagre resources if you want."

"Thanks for offering, Shiv, but I look better in black."

Police issue PPE was standard black. NHS and carers got pale blue. Both were probably useless in the current circumstances.

"Where will you take her?" The last thing Amelia wanted was to lose access to Cam when she was ready to speak.

Her friend didn't let her down. "I've found a nice little flat with a permanent minder. I'll text you the details."

"Cheers." Amelia rubbed the back of her neck.

"You okay, mate?" Carol entered some information into her phone. "I tell you what, the pubs being shut is a bloody nightmare."

"As soon as this is over…"

"With this bunch of tossers running the country?" Carol never minced her words. "We'll still be here at Christmas. Shiv, d'ya wanna take me to meet the lovely Cam?"

There was no point staying at Poppy's Place or going with Carol. She'd leave Cam to settle in for the night and give her some thinking time. Her next stop was Birmingham. She might as well check out the nail bar and surrounding area once again. Once the homeless support volunteers were about, she'd pay them a visit, too.

As soon as she reached the nail bar, she felt uneasy. There were no signs of a break-in or that the women had returned, but something just wasn't right. Anxiety crept in like a rabid dog gnawing at her senses. Amelia stopped and leaned against the alley wall next to the shop. Breathing deeply, she tried to ward off the tightness in her chest that, through experience, she expected to arrive next. It had been a while since she'd had an attack. Maybe she should have expected it with the stress of grief. As she calmed her breathing, she began to realise that this wasn't the same as usual. This felt more external; more foreboding, like being stalked by a silent predator.

Amelia glanced up and down the street, now hypersensitive to any movement or noise. She didn't spot anything out of place. In fact, the whole area was eerily quiet. Maybe it was all in her imagination.

Amelia decided to walk the canal towards Gas Street Basin. She wasn't the only one with that idea. If the nail bar was a ghost town, the towpath was a city promenade. Dog walkers, mothers pushing prams and teenagers on skateboards all hustled along for their daily exercise.

She soon discovered that Pat had meant it when she announced that Operation Caludon was finished. The narrowboat that had served them as a temporary police station was no longer moored up in its usual spot. In its place sat a rusty old boat with bags of rubbish and coal strewn across its top.

To be fair, with the factory now abandoned, there was little point in retaining it but Amelia missed it, to her surprise. She now understood how people were attracted to the murky waters. It was a slower, calmer way of life than the rest of the city would ever boast.

Beneath Birmingham's office and apartment blocks were old, working locks that gradually raised the water to the height of the basin. You could be sleeping or meeting with colleagues above without ever knowing about the busy canal beneath your feet.

Some had clearly discovered its charms. Graffiti tags decorated every corner and strut that stopped the modern buildings from crushing the lock gates and boaters below.

As Amelia walked, the more apprehensive she became. Was someone following her?

Chapter 25
Predator

The Undertaker dodged behind a pillar. He lived in the shadows. This police detective stood out in the crowd with her unnatural height and plaited auburn hair. An easy prey.

He could just tail her and let her lead him to the missing women. It would save him a job. He'd get all the glory and the reward for removing them from the street with very little effort on his part. He grinned at the thought.

It hadn't all been so simple thus far. Some jobs weren't worth doing, like the other group at the hostel. He'd passed their address to the Triads. If they wanted to pursue it, then good luck to them. He valued his freedom more than the bounty they offered.

But the women loose on the streets would be simple to dispose of. He just needed to find them.

Chapter 26
Testing Times

Whichever way you looked at it, Amelia worked outside of the rules. She was supposed to be on compassionate leave and her investigation had been ditched but, if anything, this only made Amelia work harder.

She'd searched every nook and cranny of the area around Gas Street Basin. Her next step was to question the boaters moored there. As far as she was aware, they were subject to the rules of lockdown like everyone else. They were also quite likely to have spotted a group of homeless women wandering around.

Amelia walked back to her car and opened the boot. She'd better look the part if she was doing door-to-door. She took a couple of black face masks out of a box and placed them in her pocket. Then she opened her rucksack and found her notebook and pen. She considered taking some latex gloves but decided that she could just tap on a window — and who would have touched that with virus-ridden hands?

Back at the basin, Amelia decided to start with the first boat moored up behind an abandoned-looking café. Most of its chalk signs were worn away. No one would be buying coffee or cake on the towpath in the near future.

Amelia tapped on the window of the small, dainty boat. It had a brightly painted sign on its bow: *Little Miss Daisy*. A young woman opened the hatch next to the window. "Hi," she said with a broad smile.

Amelia held out her police badge attached to a lanyard. "I'm with the police," she explained, despite the NCA insignia next to her picture. Her face was covered by a black face mask, anyway, so even if anyone bothered to look closely they'd have had a hard time identifying her.

The woman continued to smile. "I hope you haven't come to tell me I should be moving the boat."

"No, of course not."

"I'm just kidding. I'm sure you lot have got better things to do." The woman looked down for a moment and then raised her head again. "I'm Jackie. How can I help?"

For some bizarre reason, Amelia expected her to be called Daisy. She told her the tale that she'd woven on the way back to the car. It wasn't too far from the truth. "We've had reports of a group of homeless women sheltering by the canal. We're hoping to house everyone while we're in lockdown. You haven't seen them, by any chance?"

The woman squinted back up at her and bit her lip. "You know what? I have, and I did think of calling someone. Now I feel dreadful."

Amelia's heart began to race. "Can you show me where you saw them?"

"Sure, hang on a minute." Jackie closed the hatch and Little Miss Daisy rocked as she made her way to the stern of the boat. She soon appeared holding a bunch of keys with a cork ball attached.

It reminded Amelia of the time that she'd spent on *A Cut Above*. She actually missed being on the water, though probably wouldn't admit it to her colleagues. She was meant to be an all-guns-blazing city girl, far removed from the young woman in front of her dressed in a tie-dyed dress, para boots and an over-large hoodie, exuding freedom.

Jackie led her to the boaters' bins next to the wharf. They were overflowing with black bin bags and various dumped rubbish. A couple of dirty sleeping bags protruded from behind the bins. Jackie waved in their direction. "They were using those." A darkness settled over the woman like a heavy blanket. Jackie's mood was now the polar opposite to what it had been on the boat. "I know it's unbearable to think about. They ran when they saw me."

Amelia shuddered. "When was this?"

"Last night. Late, after midnight. I'd spilt the milk making hot chocolate." She grimaced. "On the boat, every smell... you know."

And Amelia did know.

She thanked Jackie. It was certainly worth returning here tonight but she was beginning to think that these women would always be just out of reach like that part of your back that needed a good scratch.

The gnawing feeling of being watched returned as soon as Jackie left to return to her boat. Amelia glanced around the wharf. The only movement was the occasional swaying of the boats, a sign that many were occupied by people obeying the stay-at-home rule. Maybe she was getting paranoid. This going-it-alone that she'd done so often — some would say too often — was affecting her brain.

What to do now? It wasn't like there was anywhere open to get a coffee and wait. It would be a few hours before darkness and any chance that the women would return. She didn't want to go home. Home meant tears that she didn't want to shed.

Just off the canal, a small supermarket

was open for business. Amelia bought four bottles of an IPA that she knew her friend liked and a bottle of red wine. She might as well go to Carol's. If you were going to Carol's, then it was best not to arrive empty-handed.

Carol Jamieson lived in a large apartment in a trendy area of the city centre. To be fair, she'd bought her flat when central city living was considered dangerous and frowned upon as not the place for young singletons to be. Carol probably liked it for the proximity to late night clubs and restaurants, anywhere she could get a drink and maybe food after hours.

Amelia followed the map on her phone to get to the apartment. There was no point in moving her car to only have to move it back to the basin later that night. She was surprised to find that she enjoyed the walk through the back streets of Birmingham. Every few minutes she peered back over her shoulder but only spotted a stray cat rifling through a pile of rubbish or the blurry headlamps of a car in the distance. Why couldn't she get past this feeling that she wasn't alone?

Carol's tall apartment block stood in front of her. It was far shabbier than the others on the boundary of the city ring road. Despite that, with dusk falling, every window was lit.

The apartment block may have been shabby but Carol's flat was modern and airy. Amelia knew that she had a regular cleaner and rarel spent time at home to make much of a mess. She'd half expected her friend to be out now and was surprised when Carol answered the intercom within moments of her pressing the button.

They soon settled in for the evening. Amelia only took sips of her drink as she knew she still had work to do later on. Carol didn't have that worry. Neither woman spoke for a long time. It was enough that they were in close proximity. It was only after her second glass of wine that Amelia realised that she was breaking the rules again by visiting someone else in their home. She couldn't even use the excuse that this was work. Guilt spread its clasping hand around her throat, nearly choking her.

"You okay, mate?" Carol asked. "You look a bit pale."

"This is why I lost my mother." Amelia waved her glass round.

"I know she was an alcoholic once, but —"

"No." Amelia stared at her glass. "Not the drink. Me... being here... not following the bloody rules again."

Carol started to laugh, a small giggle emanating from her stomach until it became raucous and unstoppable. "Jesus! If people died every time you broke the rules, this city would be deserted."

Most people outside of Carol's friendship circle might have seen this behaviour as wholly inappropriate, but Amelia wasn't offended. Instead, she smiled, not yet ready to laugh but, given time, she would be. Any time spent with her friends was healing. Amelia thought of all those who were doing the right thing and the effect it must be having on their mental health. What if you'd just lost a parent and lived alone? You'd have no one to pour out your grief to. At some point, that pressure cooker was bound to explode.

After another period of silence, Amelia's mind turned back to work. "Did you get Cam settled?"

"Yeah. One of my sergeants is spending the night with her. She's a right surly so-and-so."

"The sergeant or Cam?"

"Both, if I'm honest." Carol poured another glass of wine, emptying the bottle.

"You'll let me know if she says anything important?"

"Yeah. I'll set up a shared folder and give you access. But I doubt there'll be much over the next few days."

Amelia knew how this worked. It could be at least a week before Cam opened up, and even then she might not have anything useful to say. They needed good descriptions and names to reopen the case. If they didn't get either, Cam might still be shipped back home no matter what provisional bargains had been made.

Hours later, Amelia awoke with a start. She must have nodded off at some point. Carol had covered her with a blanket and switched off the lights, allowing her some much-needed rest. Amelia immediately groped for her phone. Unlocking it, she saw that it was 2:00 in the morning. She breathed out slowly. At least it wasn't nearly morning. There was plenty of time to walk back to the bins to see if the women had returned. She wrote a quick text to Carol thanking her for letting her stay, then reached for her things.

Outside was like a different world. It could be a scene from *Blade Runner* with rubbish flying around, very few people, and neon signs flashing. Fortunately, the council hadn't switched off the streetlamps, so Amelia could see where she was going. The last thing she wanted was to be stuck in the pitch black without a torch. If she'd been more prepared, she'd have slipped her police torch into her handbag, but she wasn't exactly thinking straight at the minute.

It wasn't long before she reached the canal. Instead of sticking to the footpath, she chose to walk the towpath. There was no sign of the women under the bridge where they'd been spotted before. There was no sign of anyone.

She reached the bins to find that there were few lights on in the moored boats at this time of night. There were no streetlamps by the boater's bins. She began to understand why they'd chosen this place to sleep. It was close enough to the water in an area they knew, and boaters weren't a risk to them. Amelia, as a boater, had befriended Julie. Or maybe it was the other way round? Maybe Julie had befriended Amelia, and maybe she wasn't the first boater that she'd spoken to? Perhaps the water attracted her, or maybe it was the slower way of life these people had compared to the city dwellers who darted around, always in a hurry to be somewhere else.

Amelia tiptoed up to the wooden fence housing the bins. As she drew closer, she heard some murmurings. She leaned against the wood and could hear faint breathing sounds. There at least one person asleep near the bins. It could, of course, be another vagrant looking for some shelter.

The last thing she wanted to do was startle the women, so she crept round to the entrance. She still couldn't make out the shapes of people although they could have been blocked by the two large industrial wheelie bins at the front. She tiptoed further into the space and, in the gloom, spotted a pair of legs sticking out from the back of one of the bins. A step closer and she made out a couple more figures.

A shriek broke the silence. One of the women must have heard her. They all shot up at the same time and must have seen that she was blocking their escape. Amelia needed to calm them immediately or they could flood past her in their bid for freedom.

"It's okay. Is Julie here? I can help you."

Not a sound, but no more movement, either. Amelia crouched down. They could barely see each other in the darkness. They were obviously weighing up their options.

"Yes. I'm here." A woman crawled from behind the furthest bin. "I know you from the bridge. Why are you following us?"

It was make-or-break time. "I'm DI Amelia Barton. I'm a police officer and I can help you. I know where the other women are and they're all safe."

There was a dull, loud thump behind Amelia. Startled, everyone turned to the entrance of the bins. Amelia jumped up and peered towards the origin of the noise. One of the boats was rocking from side to side. The rope securing its bow had come off its mooring bollard. *Had someone tripped on it? Was she being followed after all?*

Amelia turned back to the women, who were now huddled together. "It's okay. I'm just going to make a call and we'll get you somewhere safe. Somewhere safe and warm."

Pat was not too happy to be woken in the middle of the night, but she arranged for ambulances for the women, judging that it was best to get them all checked out at the hospital first. They would probably all be tested to see if they had the virus, but from what Amelia could see, they were all as healthy as could be expected after living on the streets for a while.

By the time Amelia got home, she expected everyone to be still fast asleep in bed, so was shocked to find Jola and Caitlyn cuddled up on the sofa. "Is everything okay?"

Jola nodded. "Caitlyn couldn't sleep. She's got a bit of a cough, too."

Caitlyn shuffled out of Jola's grasp and rushed towards her mother, who hugged her.

Jola stood up and grasped Amelia's shoulder. "You okay if I go up to bed?"

"Of course." Amelia took her poorly daughter to bed with her. Michal had gone back home. She didn't much care at that point if she caught it, too.

After a long lie-in, Amelia was greeted by Jola in the kitchen. "I've booked Caitlyn a test at the Ricoh."

Amelia yawned. "A test for what?"

"For COVID." Jola stared at her as though she was stupid.

"Is she up?" At some point, Caitlyn had taken herself off to her own bed.

"Yes, she's in the garden hitting stuff but she has a high temperature over 39 degrees and she's still coughing." Jola poured a cup of coffee.

"I'll take her. What time?"

The testing centre occupied the whole of the Ricoh stadium car park. There was a long queue of traffic leading to the first white tent. Caitlyn looked pale and tiny curled up in the car seat next to her. They got closer to the tent and were met by a young man in an apron, gloves, mask and shield. He held up a sign displaying a message and a phone number: PLEASE CALL THIS NUMBER. Amelia called the number and was given a set of instructions that took her to another tent further inside the cordon.

By this time, Caitlyn looked terrified. "It's okay," Amelia touched her leg. "They're just keeping everyone safe."

A woman dressed in PPE stepped out with a sign with another mobile number written underneath. When she called this one, she was asked to open her window. When Amelia did so, they dropped in a clear, plastic bag and a sheet of step-by-step instructions. The woman indicated the parking bays in front of her. "Pull up over there and follow the instructions on the sheet. When you've finished, go to the next station."

Amelia did as she was asked. She read the first instruction. *1 – Sanitise your hands.* Amelia had a small bottle on her dashboard. She squeezed some into her right hand. Caitlyn held out hers and she squeezed some into the pool she'd made with them. They both rubbed i in. *2 – Blow your nose using the tissue provided.* Caitlyn gave a strong blow into the tissue and then started to cough. Amelia glanced out the window to see all the white-suited operatives rigidly standing and starin at them. It was like something out of a horro movie. *3 – Peel off the label and stick it on the test tube.* Amelia went to do this but ended up dropping the bag on the floor. Fortunately, nothing fell out of the bag. The next step required them to take out the swab and swab the back of Caitlyn's throat.

Amelia turned to her daughter, who had stopped coughing but still had streaming eyes. "Do you want me to do this?"

Caitlyn nodded. She opened her mouth wide and then started to cough so shut it again. One of the operatives was heading for the car.

"Shall we try again?"

This time Caitlyn held her mouth open for longer but as soon as her mother touched the back of her throat, she gagged. Amelia hoped this was enough. She then tried to do the same to the other tonsil with the same result.

Caitlyn was crying by the time she attempted to stick the swab up her nostril. By this time, Amelia didn't care whether she'd done it correctly or not. She wanted this nightmare to be over for her daughter and for herself. She broke off the swab into the test tube and dropped it into another plastic bag before sealing it into a larger one.

At the next station, they were met by a man with a different sign. OPEN THE CAR WINDOW AND DROP THE PLASTIC BAG IN THE BIN.

Amelia completed this task and drove away with relief. It was a good job she hated football and rugby because there was no way she was ever coming back to the Ricoh Arena again.

The rest of the day was spent under duvets, watching films and drinking juice. Amelia couldn't have told anyone what the films were about as she checked her work phone every five minutes for emails. She wanted to make sure that all the women from the warehouse were now safe.

A couple of them were still in hospital with severe malnutrition and dehydration. Any symptoms of COVID had now passed.

Siobhan had no space for the others, so they'd been found rooms at a Salvation Army hostel. Amelia had planned to visit them, but Jola had read the rules to her and she knew that it was wise to wait for Caitlyn's test result and then to self-isolate if necessary. Maybe this was a message for her to slow down now everything was heading in the right direction.

When the positive result came through, no one was surprised. Two weeks at home sounded like an eternity to Amelia, especially since Caitlyn was now much better and no one else in the household had symptoms, but the bored young woman on Track and Trace had made it clear: no one was to leave the house for fourteen days even if they were a key worker. Amelia had already had to embarrass herself by admitting to them that she'd let her boyfriend stay over and return to his household. No doubt he was getting the call now.

Her mobile rang a few moments later to confirm it.

"How's Caitlyn?"

Nice opener, thought Amelia. "She's fine. Recovering well. So, I guess you're isolating too."

Michal laughed, a soft affectionate laugh. "It's only been a couple of days and I'm already missing you."

Amelia paused. She was missing him, but should she say that? Things were moving at a steady yet slow pace and that was how she liked it. But he'd been much more than a good friend recently. He'd been her support and she, perhaps, should admit that, at least to herself. "Strangely enough, I miss you too, and I know Caitlyn does."

"I'll Skype her later with a lesson."

So, Caitlyn gets a Skype call.

After a silent, contemplative pause, Michal said, "It'd be nice to see you, too — online, of course."

Amelia hoped he wasn't being suggestive. She was too long in the tooth for that sort of nonsense.

Michal laughed again and Amelia imagined his broad, comforting smile. "I didn't mean anything like that."

Was he reading her mind now? "Good job," she muttered.

The conversation moved on to more mundane things until it was interrupted by a couple of beeps.

Pat was trying to get through. Her first words were: "Cheun wants to talk."

Amelia fumed. She should have been interviewing Cheun, not sitting at home doing nothing. Catherine and Sean were given the honour. At least they'd met up on Teams to discuss strategy, but she knew that Cheun would lead this interview, not them. Whatever he had to say would determine their tasks and his future.

Pat patched her into the recording. She could at least hear, if not see, the rat.

He started by explaining that he couldn't tell them about the leaders of his particular gang. That would risk the life of his family back in China. But he could tell them something even bigger and, for that, he wanted to cut a deal.

Neither Catherine nor Sean prompted him with promises. *That's it, let him speak,* thought Amelia.

Cheun carried on. "We employ someone to do our dirty work. To deal with death."

"Death? How do you mean?"

Amelia knew that death was a taboo topic in China and not openly discussed. Was this why they needed a proxy?

"He gets rid of the bodies. The Undertaker." Cheun paused. Amelia imagined him grinning, as though he was pleased with himself for passing this tidbit on. "Oh, and not just for the Triads — for anyone who'll pay him."

Amelia picked up her mobile, a question burning.

Catherine asked it before she had time to dial. "Who else has he worked for?"

"The Romanian sex traffickers, drug runners, anyone in the West Midlands with a death to hide. Only he doesn't hide the bodies, he likes to put them on display."

"Fuck!" Amelia dropped the phone.

By the afternoon, the team had a good description of The Undertaker and the white van he used to carry the dead. Amelia knew in her gut that he'd worked for The Devil. This was the man who'd taunted them with the bodies of dead, trafficked women. But even worse, he'd taunted her with Chloe. What had he done with her before he'd placed her to be found?

But Amelia still had another twelve days of self-isolation. She couldn't take to the streets in search of the bastard. Instead, she spent the time getting angrier and more frustrated by the hour, leading Jola to refuse to let her anywhere in the house other than her bedroom and office. Food and drink were left on trays and her girls were given clear instructions not to disturb their mother. Like a prisoner, she had to book time to walk in the garden.

By day six, Amelia had calmed down enough to apologise for her behaviour. She'd spent the morning on intelligence work sent over by Will. She'd always thought his area of work was inanely boring, but she found it quite therapeutic to focus on searching police records for anyone of similar appearance to The Undertaker. She discounted anyone too young, too old, or already dead. Then she looked at the offences they'd committed. It wasn't likely to be a motoring offence or burglary. Sex crimes were a possibility that she didn't discount. It was, also, a possibility that he had never appeared on their radar.

What skills would this man possess? A strong stomach? Maybe. He was used to being around the dead. Had he worked in a mortuary or funeral home? Amelia ran a search on both these professions for known offenders but drew a blank. It seemed these professions weren't attractive to the criminal underclass.

It was only when she calmed down and rejoined her family that she began to think more clearly. She did an online search for funeral directors in the West Midlands and saved their telephone numbers. There were over 100 of them. Then she made a list of hospital mortuaries. She'd need to systematically ring them all. And ask what?

Another walk around the garden was in order. Most of the boxing gear had been moved to the garage except for the speedball, which hung from a pergola that Jane had bought when she was going through a gardening phase. Caitlyn's boxing gloves wouldn't fit her, but Amelia's husband had taken up boxing for all of three weeks and she vaguely remembered there was a larger pair of gloves hanging up in the garage. She went to look. Sure enough, the pair of red gloves with black laces hung from one of the wall units. She carefully undid the laces. The gloves were a comfortable fit. Her hands matched her height and were larger than those of the average woman.

Outside, she soon got into a comfortable rhythm with the speedball. Caitlyn came to join her. She got Jola to carry the punchbag back out of the garage and the two of them exercised for the next half hour. Neither spoke but they shared a great deal.

Amelia took a shower and returned to her study. She had a good idea of what her opening questions would be. The first ten calls to funeral directors drew a complete blank. Some were even affronted that their profession might attract weirdos with a fascination for death. They were quick to get Amelia off the line as they were busy people with more pressing tasks.

The eleventh call was answered by a cheery, "Hello."

Amelia gave them the same spiel as she had the others.

The woman responded quickly and resolutely, "Oh, you mean Jason."

Amelia tapped her pen on her notepad. "Jason?"

"Yeah. He didn't last long."

"Why is that?"

"He was too interested. You know, in the bodies, I mean."

"In what way?"

"Well, he was always in there staring at them as they were being prepared... for burial, like."

"Staring at them?"

"Yeah, any excuse. And we found him touching the bodies a couple of times. He was only supposed to clean."

"He was employed as a cleaner?"

"And he wasn't much good at that."

Amelia phoned more on her list and a few had heard of Jason, although occasionally he was a James or a Jamie and he had different surnames all starting with a B. She now had a possible suspect. They just had to find him.

The rest of the time spent in isolation

made Amelia realise that she would never survive prison. It drove her steadily bonkers. Much as she loved her children, she was never meant to be a full-time mother. She enjoyed boxing with Caitlyn, talking about forensics with Becky and playing with Callum's toys. He just watched as she rebuilt his castle for the tenth time after he'd destroyed it with a trebuchet. It made her feel for those who were shielding. She was fortunate not to have any health issues.

Her team had visited all the addresses provided for Jason. He wasn't at any of them. It seemed that he changed his address as often as his place of work. But they did have a more detailed description and a photofit picture now. They thought they had a number plate for his vehicle, but he'd scrapped that particular one and moved on to another.

It was a waiting game, a game of chance as they waited for The Undertaker to play his next card. Amelia weighed up what other events he could have been responsible for. Was he the one who had tried to break in at Poppy's Place? The build and height were similar.

After another session on the speedball, Amelia remembered something else. Maybe she'd met Jason? Was he the guy with the van working with the homeless charity? The photofit hadn't led her to think of him. What was the difference? The guy she had spoken to had thin, sparse hair. The guy in the photofit had curly, shoulder-length hair. But if you took that out of the picture, their features were very similar. Maybe he once wore a wig or had just aged quickly.

Amelia rang the church but no one answered. She looked up the charity. It was only listed as having an office number. She tried it but, as expected, no one answered. The answerphone did list a mobile, but she had no joy with that either.

Tomorrow was freedom day. She could wait until then to go looking for the volunteers.

They spent their last day under lock and key in all-day-party mode. Jola laid out all the food left in the house as a buffet for everyone to snack on. She planned to do a huge shop the next day and had arranged for Becky to have Callum in the morning to do so. Then Jola had planned a long walk for everyone in the afternoon. Amelia would be at work and had already warned them that they wouldn't see her for the whole day and evening, at least.

Despite Birmingham City Council having housed many of the homeless in local hostels and hotels, there was still a need for the soup run. Amelia found Stephen Standege loading up his trolley with rolls outside St Michael's Church.

"You again," he muttered. "Not found your women yet?"

"As it happens, we have." *No thanks to you*, she thought. "I've come to ask you about Jason, the van driver."

"Jason?"

"Or he could be going by James or Jamie."

Stephen added another tray to his trolley. "Nope. No one I know."

Amelia reached into her pocket and pulled out a crumpled E-fit picture. "This guy, though when I saw him, he was balding."

Stephen glanced at the picture. "Oh, him. He's not been with us for a while."

"But he did volunteer?"

'Yeah, only for a few nights. Some don't stick around. It was useful having his van, though, as I didn't have to do lots of trips with my car to get supplies."

"What name did he go by, and do you have any contact details?"

Stephen shrugged. "Somewhere, maybe at home."

Amelia might have waited until later for it, but he was starting to ignore her. "Well, then, you're going to have to come with me to get it."

"I've got these to give out."

Amelia motioned to one of the other volunteers to come and get the truck. "Not tonight."

Stephen lived in Handsworth. It would usually take about twenty-five minutes longer to get there in rush hour. The one positive about lockdown was that it shaved time off any journey, so twenty minutes later they both pulled up at a three-storey apartment block. Stephen's flat was on the ground floor. Amelia waited until he'd let himself in before leaving the car.

The first thing that struck her about the apartment was the sheer number of books. Stephen must be an avid reader. Every surface supported precarious piles of novels and each wall was covered in shelving holding hundreds more.

The only time Amelia ever read was at Christmas, and even then it was usually a novel that Becky had chosen for her. It had been a joke first organised by Joe. "The morning of Boxing Day should be for staying in bed and reading." Becky wanted this to carry on after his death. Even if Amelia had to work at Christmas, they still found an hour or two to stop and read. The problem was that she rarely finished the book before Easter.

Stephen rummaged through a filing cabinet in his spare bedroom, which he used as an office. Amelia wondered if this arrangement was just for the duration of the pandemic or if the charity had no proper base. He took out a thin file and laid it open on the desk. Then he picked up a pen and wrote something on a yellow sticky note. He handed the note to Amelia. "This is the address he gave me."

"Have you got a phone number?" Amelia asked.

Stephen tutted and took the note back. He scribbled on it. "Here." He passed the note back and put the pen back in a plain metal pencil pot.

"Thanks." Amelia nearly added, "It wasn't hard, was it?" Instead, she decided to give him some slack. "Have you been working in the field long?"

Stephen stared down at the desk. "Ten years. I was homeless myself. So I know."

"Must've been tough."

He shrugged, still not looking at Amelia. "It would've been easier if we weren't hassled all the time."

"By the police?"

"And the council."

So this was why he was so abrupt. "Not my area."

"What are you going to do with the women you found? Deport them?"

Amelia sighed, "I don't make those decisions. At least they're safe now."

Stephen rose and moved towards the door before muttering, "Are they?"

Maybe he was right. "Safer" might be a better description.

The address on the sticky note was only a few miles away. She could drive there before it got dark to at least check it out and see if there was a white van parked nearby.

As she put the key in the ignition, her hands began to tremble. She tried again and still couldn't get the key to go in. "For fuck's sake!" She covered her face with her hands and began to sob.

Deep down, she told herself that she needed to pull herself together. This was ridiculous. What if someone saw her? She reached for her bag and found a packet of tissues, blew her nose, wiped her eyes and took a deep breath.

Then she tried to start the car again. This time, she was successful. Strangely, she now felt calmer and back in control. It was a though the last ten minutes or so had never happened.

In front of the address stood a TO LET sign. Amelia didn't need to get out of the ca to see that the property was empty. She noted down the letting agent's name so she could ring in the morning to see if they had a forwarding address for Jason or whatever name he was using. But she didn't expect to get an joy from that.

Jason didn't seem to stay anywhere long. He knew how to not get caught.

Chapter 28
Julie

Other NCA officers had been sent to interview the women rescued from the Birmingham warehouse. Each was shown an e-fit of Jason. Only Cam and Julie — whose name, Amelia had learned, was actually Li — showed any recognition of the man. Cam recalled that he'd turned up on the day that some of the ill women were taken from the factory. She was told that they were being segregated to avoid infecting everyone else. Amelia was pretty sure that wasn't what happened. How long would it be before their bodies showed up?

She decided to visit Julie, who had a room at the Sally Army hostel in Coventry.

Julie seemed pleased to see her. Her eyes lit up above the blue face mask she wore when Amelia entered the tv room. It was currently closed for residents, but the centre manager opened it up for them. Amelia knew the rooms here were tiny but at least had ensuite facilities. She couldn't imagine how hard it was for residents without any of the usual amenities like the lounge and the games room. It was a mixed hostel and, for some women who were survivors of sex trafficking, this was a real concern. This was the reason why Amelia supported Poppy's Place.

Julie held her hands out but kept the two meters between them. She nodded and said, "Thank you."

Amelia smiled, then wondered if she should have a face mask on. "For what?"

"Saving me." Julie paused. "And the others... for saving us."

"It's my job." Amelia reached into her

bag and took out the e-fit. She placed it on the coffee table between them. "Do you remember this man?"

Julie glanced at the photo. "Yes. He came to the factory."

"Tell me about that."

Julie sighed and screwed up her eyes. "It was after some of the women started coughing. Cheun panicked. He kept ringing people and shouting at them to help."

"Did you know about the virus?" Amelia wondered how scared the women were and what they'd been told.

"Not really... but we heard people talking, both the men who watched over us and the punters."

Punters. These women knew what their role was at the factory. They even knew the western terms.

Julie continued. "We knew there was an illness that started in China and people were dying."

They must have been petrified. "What happened when this man turned up?" Amelia tapped on the picture.

"Cheun and the man talked outside for quite a while. We didn't hear what they said but everyone seemed to know it wasn't a normal discussion."

A normal discussion would, no doubt, be about what was on offer at the factory and the cost.

"Then the man came into our sleeping area. We usually met them upstairs. So, we knew something was wrong." Julie stopped and rubbed her palms on her trousers.

"What happened next?"

"Cheun pointed at the sickest women and

the man just nodded. Then all the sick ones were wrapped up in their blankets."

"Go on."

"Their heads were covered, too... like they were dead."

"But they were still alive?"

"Yes. Cheun and the other men didn't want to carry them. This man," Julie pointed to the picture, "shouted at them in English. Something like – get the fuck on with it. Then they left and we never saw them again."

"The women, you mean?"

"Yes. They never came back."

Neither woman spoke until Julie said, "They're dead, aren't they?"

"Yes, I think so." Amelia stood to leave.

Julie looked up at her. "I saw him again."

Amelia sat back down. "When?"

"By the canal. The night you found us. I'm sure it was him. He got out of a white van next to the bridge by the pub. We all hid as quickly as we could... He didn't see us, I think."

Thank God for that, Amelia thought.

Amelia planned to drive to the safe house where Cam was staying but, before she could start her car, her mobile rang. It was Jola. "You must come home. Straight away."

Amelia clutched the phone. "Why, what's happened?"

"It's Becky."

Amelia didn't wait to hear anymore. She started the car and raced home.

She found Caitlyn in the front room with Callum when she entered the house. They were playing with his cars. Caitlyn looked up and smiled at her mother. There was no sign of any issues there.

Amelia couldn't find Jola or Becky downstairs, so she headed up.

She found her daughter and Jola in the bathroom. Becky's head was over the toilet and Jola was holding her hair back as she vomited violently.

"What's happened? Are you ill?"

"Becky thought it was a good idea to drink a bottle of vodka."

Amelia let that sink in. They didn't allow alcohol in the house as their grandmother had been an alcoholic, so Becky would have had to leave the house to get it. Why had she done it, though?

Of course, Amelia knew why. This was grief in its purest form. She waited until Becky stopped retching and asked Jola to leave. Then she washed her daughter's face, wrapped her in a blanket and took her to bed. When she had fallen asleep, Amelia removed her arm from around her and went to find a bowl, which she placed next to Becky's bed. She sat next to her for a while, watching the slow rise and fall of her chest as she breathed. It reminded Amelia of all the times she'd worked late and arrived home to find the girls in bed. She would always sneak into their room to check on them.

Everyone was in the kitchen when Amelia came downstairs. They were eating lunch, which only served to remind Amelia how early it was Becky must have woken up and started drinking What had led her to do that?

Amelia didn't say anything, just ate what she was offered. She didn't want to talk to

Jola about what had happened in front of Caitlyn and Callum, who were eating their tuna sandwiches in silence, savouring each mouthful. Amelia felt like she was chewing cardboard.

As soon as they had finished, Callum and Caitlyn left the table and went to play outside.

Jola didn't look up. Amelia understood why she was embarrassed. This had happened on her watch.

"Did you know she was drinking?"

Jola looked up straight at Amelia. "No."

Amelia believed her. "Where did she get it — the vodka?"

Jola shrugged. "She must've gone to the shop before we got up."

There was a 24/7 garage at the end of the road. But how would they have mistaken her daughter for eighteen? In Amelia's head, Becky was still a baby but, of course, her daughter was nearly seventeen, a sixth former. She could easily be mistaken for eighteen or older.

Amelia put her head in her hands. "I'm sorry, Jola. This is my fault. I should've known she was in pain."

Jola took hold of Amelia's hand. "We're all in pain."

It was time to let go. Amelia cried. Heavy, shoulder wracking sobs. Jola held her hand until she stopped.

After the sandwich and a coffee, Amelia began to feel human again. Becky was still sleeping. Amelia rang Carol and put off the interview with Cam to the next day. She then rang Michal, in need of some emotional support. He wanted to drive round immediately but she put him off, too. She didn't feel as though she deserved any sympathy since she hadn't spotted that Becky wasn't coping.

Then, of course, there was Caitlyn. Becky had no way of voicing her grief and Caitlyn was even younger than her sister. How would she voice hers?

Amelia found Caitlyn in the garage maintaining a solid rhythm of hits on the punchball. In between punches, she bounced from foot to foot. When she noticed her mother, she stopped and smiled. "Is Becky feeling better?"

Amelia sat down in one of the old garden chairs that weren't good enough for the patio "Yes, she must have eaten something dodgy."

Caitlyn gave her a quizzical look. Maybe she was old enough to understand what was really going on. Amelia asked, "Are you okay?

Caitlyn raised the gloves to her face, guarding her mouth. "Sure."

"It's okay if you're not. We all miss her, you know."

"I know. I just wish I'd gone to the funeral to say goodbye."

Amelia felt a knot tighten in her stomach. "It looks like it might rain. Get your coat."

It was only a short drive to the crematorium. They stopped at the garage for a bunch of flowers on the way. They arrived a few minutes before Michal, who had agreed to meet them outside. There was a wooden bench next to the memorial plaques, so they sat dow there. No one spoke much. Caitlyn kept her eyes shut as though saying a silent prayer. Michal held Amelia's hand. After almost an hour, Caitlyn stood up and placed the bouquet on the grass in front of them. The plaque commemorating her grandmother hadn't yet been placed at the crematorium, but this was as suitable a place as any to say goodbye.

Becky had made it downstairs when they got home. She looked sheepish, pulling a cover up to her neck on the sofa. The television was on and tuned to a Netflix series that Amelia didn't know the name of.

Amelia told Caitlyn to join her brother and Jola in the garden before turning to her elder daughter. "You gave us a bit of a scare."

Becky tried to sit up a little and clutched her head.

Serves you right, thought Amelia.

"I'm sorry, Mum. I won't do that again."

Amelia smiled. "Yes, you will, many times." *But hopefully with friends, and not on your own.*

"I... I just felt so awful..." Becky started to cry.

Amelia sat next to her and hugged her. "We're all missing your nan. It's okay."

She had lots of questions, such as: Where did you get the vodka? And why vodka? Why not speak to us? But none of them seemed important at that moment. It had happened, and Becky was recovering.

By the evening, everyone had returned to their normal family habits and personal spaces. Callum had his bath and Amelia managed to read him a book for a change. He was now sound asleep. Caitlyn had returned to the garage. Becky had her science textbook out and was copying up some notes. Jola was reading in the armchair and Amelia had returned to the study.

She added the notes from that morning's interview with Julie to a shared document file. As she was typing, she noticed that a note had been attached by Catherine. Julie had called the office and asked for Amelia. Amelia had left her a card that morning. It had her mobile number on, so she was surprised that Julie hadn't called that number. But then she checked her phone and found that it was on silent. She'd missed calls from Julie, Catherine and Michal.

She called Julie first, who answered on the second ring. "You've got to come. I'm scared."

"Of what?"

"He knows where I am, I'm sure." Julie spluttered a few more words that Amelia couldn't grasp.

"Slow down, I can't catch what you're saying."

"That man. The one you showed me. I've seen him... here."

"At the hostel?"

"On the road outside... when I went for a walk."

"Outside the hostel? When?"

"An hour ago... maybe more... come quick, please."

The local police would get there faster so Amelia messaged them, but when she arrived at the hostel there was no one outside, not even a patrol car. She showed her ID at the front desk. The volunteer on duty didn't look up from his newspaper, just nodded towards the lounge.

In the lounge, a uniformed police officer was sitting with Julie, taking her statement. "Can you describe the man?"

Julie looked up at Amelia. "She knows..."

"It's okay, I'll take over." Amelia sat down and the uniformed officer closed his notebook.

Before Amelia could say anything, Julie shouted, "I've got to be moved from here – now!"

"I can't –"

"I mean it. I can't stay here any longer. You move me now."

The problem was that there wasn't anywhere for her to go. If she contacted Siobhan, she'd have a hissy fit and it was unlikely that Julie would qualify for PPU support. Her status was not the same as Cam's, who was as much a suspect as a victim. They'd want to keep Cam close to ensure that she didn't do a runner, as much as they didn't want her to be discovered by the Triads.

"I'm not speaking to you again until you move me or I'll just run."

Amelia pondered this. They didn't really need Julie. That was the problem. She'd probably be deported as soon as they processed her referral and her forty-five-day reflection period was completed. In some ways, she'd be better off running, but Amelia couldn't tell her that.

"I'll see what I can do, but it won't be tonight."

Julie sighed and placed her hands in her lap. "Then someone will have to stay here and protect me."

Amelia gestured at the uniformed officer. "We'll get the local force to keep an eye on the hostel."

"Sure." The officer moved towards the door, mumbling into his radio.

Amelia waited for a few minutes before she spoke again. "Where did you spot him?"

"Who?" Julie asked, confused.

"The guy from the factory. Where did you see him?"

"I went to the shop. I needed some tobacco. He followed me, so I ran." Julie bit her lip.

"And you're sure it was him?"

"Of course. Don't you believe me?"

Amelia hesitated. She did believe her, but there was no point getting her more upset and frightened. Thinking about it, maybe he was following her, too. Maybe that was why she'd been feeling so on edge.

"I believe you thought it was him."

Julie seemed satisfied with that. Perhaps she didn't pick up on the nuance.

Julie started to pull at her sweatshirt sleeve. "I want to go home."

"Home?"

"Back to Vietnam... back to my kids."

"You have kids?"

Julie pursed her lips. "You don't believe that, either."

"Yes, of course I do."

Julie wouldn't be the first trafficked woman to leave her kids with relatives in the hope of finding work in the UK. Once she was earning, she may well have hoped they could join her. "What have you got?"

"Two girls, ten and eight."

"I've got two girls... and a baby boy." Well, to be fair, he was a toddler.

Julie smiled. "And you want the best for them, too. But that's not here. Here is shit.'

Amelia wasn't going to deny it. She'd never be mistaken for a tourist ambassador for the Midlands. "I'll see what I can do. You may need to stay until lockdown's over."

Julie nodded, maybe thinking about all the women who hadn't survived because of this pandemic. But then they didn't actually have any evidence yet that the other women from the warehouse were dead, only that they were taken away by this man who fixed things… fixed things usually when there had been a murder.

If Julie was at risk, what did that mean for Cam and the other women? Amelia spoke to Carol and warned her that Cam might need extr protection. She already had an officer with her at all times, unlike Julie, but she was i a house with few people around, whereas Julie was in a hostel with round-the-clock security The other women were at Poppy's, and Jason ha already discovered that they were covered by high level of protection. It wasn't impenetrable, but he hadn't been back to try again. Yet.

What's so special about this group of women? Amelia wondered.

Jason wouldn't be looking for them unles he'd been offered a large bounty to do so. Amelia hated to say it but, from the agency's point of view, these were just average trafficked women. They were only worth what the traffickers could sell them for. They wer worth nothing dead or in the custody of the authorities, police or otherwise. What had they heard or seen that made them so valuable Valuable dead, that was.

Amelia needed to speak to Cam but, befor she did that, she felt the need to tie up som loose ends. The whole case felt too much like one of those string puzzles in a child's activity book where you follow the string to see whose kite it is. So many strings were dangling in the air.

She needed to review all the murders tha Jason had possibly staged and decide if there was a link between The Devil and the Triads who were trafficking Cam and Julie.

The best place to start was back at WMROC. Amelia stopped at a corner shop on the way to pick up some milk and snacks. The last time she'd been at the office, very few people were there. It might be the perfect place for concentrating on what she needed to do, but it was unlikely that anyone would have kept the fridge stocked up.

Five files waited unopened on Amelia's desk, four of them Eastern European victims of The Devil, and the other Chloe's. Next to them were the descriptions of the missing women from the factory. All of these were possibly linked to Jason. They'd all been moved from their place of death. The Eastern European women had been displayed so that they would eventually be found, three of them in or near disused factories and one in a park. Amelia wondered what had prompted the change.

Did the killer determine where they would be disposed of or was that down to Jason? Did he call the shots? Was he just given a short brief to place them somewhere they'd be found quickly? It was highly likely that The Devil didn't want Chloe to be found quickly. Maybe Jason was told to bury her but later decided, after The Devil had been killed, to finally give her up? Perhaps it was Jason that enjoyed the discovery of the bodies? Maybe that was all down to him. Did he watch them being discovered? Did he watch the police recovery operation as they studied the body in situ and then removed it to the morgue?

Amelia opened the first file and tried to recall the woman and how she'd been found. She thought back to that day and remembered how rude DI Branfield had been. She couldn't be side-tracked by him despite the continued delays to the court date due to the bloody virus. Then she remembered how Chloe had reacted to seeing her first body. *But was anybody else there?*

Amelia couldn't recall anyone.

She moved on to the next file. A younger woman, the one Amelia was convinced had been killed as a direct message to her to stop investigating. Again, this woman hadn't been murdered at her final resting place.

The third body had been placed in a park. Clearly, Jason had wanted her to be found quickly. Was that The Devil's intention, too? Had he given the instruction to put these women on show? Did they need to be found the following morning? For what reason? Why didn't he just have them buried?

Of course, The Devil had loved to use his reputation to frighten and keep other trafficked women in their place. It was how he stopped them from running away, though he beat them, too. Or maybe he was warning Branfield that he could finish him at any time? Or perhaps Branfield enjoyed the show, being the lead officer on the case? It was a game for them both. Did Jason just follow their instructions by finding a place to display the bodies ready for them to be found the next morning?

Recalling the details of each of the murders brought Amelia no closer to understanding what motivated Jason or what his role was. Instead, there were just more questions, particularly regarding Chloe's death. What led him to bury her and then freeze her afterwards? Had he been told to bury her? Did he have to do that and send photos to prove it, and later chose to dig her up and put her on show after Davies' death? Perhaps someone else was pulling the strings — an undiscovered puppeteer?

Amelia placed all the folders in a pile, only then noticing a sticky note that had been added to the first dead woman's file, updated online 6/4/20 by Suzanna Curiova, a Slovakian police sergeant.

Amelia fired up her laptop. Amelia sighed. The officer had worked diligently to discover the identity not only of the first victim but also the other three. Each of the women now had a name and families who could bury them. This was wonderful news and Amelia made a note to contact the officer to thank her.

Then Amelia shifted her attention to the missing Vietnamese women. Why hadn't they been put on show? Cheun had said that The Undertaker liked to put dead women on display. Therefore, he must have known about the Eastern European women as none of the missing South-East Asian women had been found yet. So, had the Triads worked with Davies? Or was there another connection that they'd missed? Davies was dead and Branfield was in prison. Could another person or people be working with local OCGs across the Midlands?

Amelia sat with her head in her hands. All she had now was more questions. She needed to speak to Cam and Cheun.

Cheun had been moved to a prison fifteen miles away. Amelia completed an application to speak to him. It wouldn't be today. Under normal circumstances, she'd have to wait twenty-four hours. Family visitors weren't allowed to enter prisons due to COVID restrictions. Amelia knew her request would be granted as it was part of an existing case, even if it had been shelved for now. She would wait.

Amelia found herself outside a terraced house on a nondescript street in Coventry. The front door was opened by a plain-clothes detective who was expecting Amelia. She nodded to her and stood aside to let her in.

Cam was sitting with her feet up on a shabby, leather sofa. She smiled when Amelia entered the room.

Amelia sat on the only other chair in the room and took out a notebook. Cam's smile waned. Maybe she thought this was a social visit.

After taking the top off her pen, Amelia said, "I need you to tell me more about the gangmasters."

Cam shook her head. "No. I've told you all I know."

"We need evidence to prove you weren't directly involved in the trafficking of women. At the moment, we don't have that. You could end up in prison for a very long time, Cam."

Cam pulled her legs tighter to her chest and hugged them. Gone was the image of a tough madam in control of the women below her. However, she stayed silent, building an impenetrable wall between them.

Amelia needed to push more of her buttons. "I don't know what you've heard, but you'll need to be damned tough to survive. British prisons aren't as soft as they're made out to be. If the missing women turn up dead, then you could end up as an inmate on a murder charge." How many more straws could she clutch at?

Cam bit her lip but still said nothing.

Amelia pushed on. "Do you have family?" Maybe like Julie, Cam had a child at home.

Cam ran her hand through her long black hair. "My mother. That's all."

"Where is she?"

"Back home near Hanoi." Cam pulled her hair up away from her face. "She lives with her sister in a small village. I try and get money to her but it's not much. Not enough... never enough."

"Did you get extra for running the nail parlour?"

Cam nodded. "A little."

"What about the other women? Were they paid? Did they get to send money home?"

Cam shook her head. "They hadn't paid off their trip yet."

"But you had?"

She sighed. "Not exactly."

Amelia closed her notebook. "You've got to see it from our point of view. You're the only woman who got paid. You ran the nail bar and got to send money home, while the rest of the women were forced to work for nothing and sleep with strangers."

"I didn't hurt them." Cam threw her arms in the air and covered her face with her hands.

"But you were employed by the gang. How are you any different to Cheun and the rest?" Amelia opened her notebook. "You've got to give us something or I'll have to charge you with trafficking offences."

Cam sat motionless with her hands still covering her face.

"Cam," Amelia sat forward, "you've got to help yourself."

In a quiet voice, Cam muttered, "But I don't know anything."

"Tell me about the gangmasters. All of them, including visitors."

Cam reeled off the names of the men at the factory. These were nothing new.

"And the visitors?"

She then described Jason. Without lookin up, she said, "They were dead."

"Who?"

"The missing women you were looking for. They died in their sleep."

Even in their malnourished state, it was unlikely that they would all die, and certainly not at the same time.

"How did they die? And don't lie to me, Cam. COVID wouldn't have killed them that suddenly."

Cam looked up and stared straight at Amelia. "The boss killed them. He told Cheun to give them sleeping tablets."

"How many sleeping tablets?"

"He brought them with him. Packets and packets of them to keep them quiet. They wouldn't stop coughing and were putting the punters off."

"You still had men coming to the factory for sex?" More fool them if they contracted more than a sexually transmitted disease.

"Yes. Not as many, but some."

Cam gave her a description of the head trafficker. At least Amelia could share it with some of her colleagues and – just maybe they could get someone higher up the food chain and a potential murderer.

"Thank you, Cam. This will help."

"There's more. But I need immunity. I mean, real immunity so I can stay and work here and help my family. A new identity, the lot."

"Go on." Amelia couldn't promise anything.

"Not until I have something to sign. Something legal."

Chapter 30
Kidnap

Amelia left the safe house wondering how she'd manage to turn Cam. The information she'd gathered so far would help Cam's case, but she couldn't make any promises without first talking to Pat, and that would mean explaining why she'd carried on investigating the case when it had been closed.

When she got home, she tried contacting Pat on Teams but got no answer. While she waited for Pat to return her call, she checked in with her family. Becky seemed much more settled. She was sitting at the dining room table completing some schoolwork. She looked up at her mum and smiled.

"How's it going?" Amelia asked.

"Okay, but it's not as good reading about experiments instead of doing them yourself."

At least Becky was seeing her teachers online now. At the start, Becky had just been given some worksheets to do. But Amelia understood that this was all very hard on their teachers, too. She sometimes wished that she'd played the key worker card and kept the girls in school, but circumstances had been different then. They had Jola, after all, and could stay at home. It was only fair that others should get the places and, the fewer children attended school, the safer it was.

Amelia hugged her daughter and went in search of Caitlyn. She half expected to find her in the garden, physical activity always taking priority over the workbook that her school had sent. She'd probably finished it by now, anyway.

Instead, she found Caitlyn with Jola in

the kitchen, making bread. Amelia must have looked surprised. Caitlyn grinned at her and said, "It was either this or more maths. Jola thinks I've got kneader's arms."

"Must be all that boxing." Jola ruffled her daughter's hair.

Callum sat at the table playing with a bowl of seeds that Amelia hoped weren't intended for the bread. She reached for him but was interrupted by her mobile phone vibrating in her pocket. She took it out and saw it was Pat.

"I'll leave you to it," she said and went back to her office.

Amelia managed to get to her laptop in time to answer. Pat looked older on the screen, her hair dishevelled and she wore jeans and a T-shirt rather than work clothes, but it was the lack of make-up that aged her.

Without any pleasantries, Amelia launched into telling her boss what Cam had revealed.

Pat held back any admonishment for Amelia's continued work on the case. Instead, she said, "Good work," but she followed that with, "I doubt we'll be able to offer Cam much. Things aren't normal at the moment. Our online work and county lines take priority at the minute."

"What do you mean? These are top-level OCG!"

"Protecting the public in the 'here and now' comes first. You know that, Amelia. We've got limited staff and even more limited resources."

"Can't we at least offer her a deal and see what she has to say?"

Pat shrugged. "The women aren't at risk. We haven't found the bodies of any dead women so there's no point in taking it further for now. Circulate the description of the Triad leader and see if you can get a formal ID, but apart from that we should probably drop it."

Amelia slammed her hand down on the desk out of sight of her boss. But she couldn't hide the mouthed "*Fuck!*"

"I've emailed you a new assignment. Finish up the paperwork on this and get started on your new tasks. We can catch up on it in the morning briefing." Pat cut the call.

It took Amelia a while to check her emails and, when she did, she avoided the new one from Pat. She would open it when she'd calmed down.

There was one person who could help, one person who might be able to get some extra security for Cam so that it would at least appear that they were taking her request seriously — and that was Carol Jamieson. Amelia reached for her phone and called her friend.

Carol seemed pleased to hear from her. She suggested they meet at the safe house so that Carol could assess what extras they could offer. It was all bollocks really, as all she'd be able to do was to move her to another house or maybe provide her with an extra bodyguard. She couldn't make any promises about her long-term safety or offer any immunity from prosecution. But it was better than nothing and perhaps they could get further revelations from Cam in the meantime.

Amelia grabbed her coat and bag. Outside, the rain was pouring down, giving the street a much-needed scrub after the dry spell of the previous few weeks. At least they had a garden. Amelia couldn't imagine how women coped teaching their kids in tiny flats with little outdoor space. They weren't even supposed to take them to the park. All the play equipment had been taped off, anyway. There were few people unaffected by the virus. Many, like Amelia, had lost family and friends, so perhaps a few months of being locked down would eventually be worth it.

She arrived at the safe house before Carol and parked a few doors away. The rain was falling in sheets, bouncing off the pavement, the drains struggling to cope with the deluge. Amelia waited for a few minutes to see if it would subside. The coat she wore would barely keep out a shower and her court shoes weren't much better. She did have some trainers on the back seat of the car, so she reached over and grabbed them, pleased that she hadn't left them in the boot.

The rain showed no signs of stopping or even slowing down so Amelia prepared herself to run to the front door. She grabbed her bag and opened the car door. Holding the bag over her head, she managed to get out of the car and shut the door with her bottom. She then darted to the safe house, dodging the worst of the puddles.

She knocked hard on the front door and waited, expecting it to be opened quickly by the officer guarding Cam, particularly since she'd rung ahead to let him know she was coming. But no one came to the door, so she knocked again, harder this time. Her bag wasn't keeping much of the rain off and she cursed under her breath.

Still no one answered.

Bending down, she peered through the letterbox but couldn't see anything inside, the storm making the hall dark and gloomy.

What to do next? She considered ringing Carol. This wasn't right. She swiped to find her number but before she could dial, she heard a loud bang from inside the house.

Amelia remembered that there was a back entry to the house. She'd spotted it when she used the downstairs toilet. She peered down the street. There was a gap between the house a short distance from her car. She dashed towards it. She was out of the rain for a few seconds but there was no time to relish that. She needed to find a way into the backyard of the safe house. Her bag banged against her le as she ran, counting down the houses until sh found the right gate. She rattled it. It was locked.

Amelia kicked the gate hard near to its lock but it was far less weak and dilapidated than those of its neighbours. She kicked it again and it flew open. Amelia didn't care that she was alerting whoever was in the hous to her presence. Cam's safety was more important.

The body of a man lay across the thin strip of lawn. Amelia knelt down and felt for a pulse. Nothing. She recognised him as the officer who had been protecting the house. Th back of his head was wet, slick with blood.

She needed to be quick. Whoever was inside knew she was here and may well have made a run for it out of the front of the house. It wasn't as though they had the place surrounded.

The back door leading to the kitchen stood open. Amelia searched for a weapon. A partially filled knife block stood next to th bread bin. She grabbed the largest of the

remaining knives before opening the door into
the hall.

Silence.

At least the front door was shut, which
hopefully meant that whoever was in the house
hadn't fled. But that meant that they were
still here.

Without making a sound, Amelia pushed
open the living room door. The contents of a
bookshelf lay strewn across the floor. Glass
from a broken vase crunched underfoot. There
were clear signs of a struggle but the room
was empty. There was no sign of Cam and or the
person who had taken her.

Before Amelia could investigate the rest
of the house, there was a loud rap on the
front door, making Amelia jump. She waited a
moment to see if anyone else stirred. When she
heard nothing, she went to the door. She
opened it to find Carol on the doorstep, her
short blonde hair stuck to her forehead. "You
took your time."

Amelia opened the door and led Carol into
the living room. "I think we're too late."

"What the fu...?" Carol's eyes scoured
the room. "What the fuck's happened here?
Where's Cam?"

Chapter 31
Negotiation

Crime scene technicians took over. The house was soon swarming with large numbers of officers busy with clearly defined tasks. Amelia and Carol escaped to Amelia's car.

Carol opened the glove compartment. "I don't suppose you've got anything to warm us up…"

Amelia knew what she meant. She shut the compartment, nearly trapping her friend's fingers. "Er, no."

"Fuck." Carol sat back in the passenger seat. "He had a young family. It's a bloody nightmare."

"Who's going to tell them?" Amelia worried it would be her friend.

"The Super's doing it."

Amelia nodded. That made sense. They'd probably be worried that Carol would smell of booze. Lockdown had hit her hard with the pubs shut. Amelia knew her friend was drinking more than usual. She'd heard the rumours and now felt dreadful that she hadn't been there for her. But she had her own problems, too.

"I'm thinking of driving back to PPU. Why don't you meet me there and we can see if they've found any signs of the hostage-taker on CCTV?" Carol reached for the door handle. What she was really saying was *I've got booze in my car and I need it*.

Amelia didn't think that would help but she wasn't Carol's keeper. "Sure. We've got to find Cam or what's the fucking point?"

Carol paused. "What do you mean?"

Amelia raised her arms. "Of any of this. If we can't shut down the OCG ops, why do we even bother?"

"You've managed to get so many women to safety."

"And at what cost? Your officer over there. Cam, possibly? It's so rare that we get those at the top and, yeah, we might save one or two women, but they're instantly replaced by more. And those bastards just get away with it."

Carol nodded. She could see her point.

"This is me. Done." Amelia turned her key in the ignition, giving Carol her cue to go to her own car.

Once at PPU, Amelia's mood changed. Carol's team had managed to track a white van from the safe house. It had stopped in Birmingham city centre not far away from the factory where the women had been kept.

The first thing that crossed Amelia's mind was that this was where he was going to kill and display the body. There was no doubt in her mind that the kidnapper was Jason and that he had taken Cam to keep her quiet. There was no sign that he'd killed her at the safe house, so maybe there was still a chance she could be saved.

Amelia wanted to leave there and then but was forced to wait for a team to assemble before heading for the warehouse.

The team was quickly briefed in the yard at the PPU and Amelia was assigned to one of the vans — another thirty minutes wasted. The only hope for Cam now was that Jason had not killed her straight away.

Amelia glanced at the other officers in

the van. Most of them were young men. They travelled in silence, no doubt aware of what had happened to their colleague. It was always personal when another officer was killed and this worried Amelia. They were more likely to go after the perpetrator than be concerned with protecting Cam. That was going to be her job.

The van slowed as it approached the factory, which appeared unremarkable from the road – just another dirty, derelict brick building with broken windows that winked in the early evening sun.

The teams disembarked from the van and waited for their instructions. Amelia went in search of the chief negotiator

She recognised the officer from a distance. DI Paul Moreton had trained with Amelia at Hendon. He was nice enough, quick-witted and intelligent. The last time she'd spoken to him, he had been an FLO. Family Liaison was often seen as a sideways move, but Amelia knew that this role was crucial and one of the most important in the force.

Amelia stood next to him and stared up at the building. Paul turned towards her. "Amelia. Good to see you."

"You too. Do we know if they're in there?"

Paul raised a set of binoculars. "We've spotted a man and a woman. They're currently on the second floor."

"And the woman – she's alive?" Amelia moved closer to Paul.

He lowered the lenses. "For now."

Amelia mumbled, "Thank you," to no one in particular.

"We're going to assemble a team at each

exit and a couple of armed officers in that building there." He pointed at a small outbuilding on the other side of the road. "Then we'll see if he'll talk to us."

"Do you think he's armed?"

"We've no way of knowing, so it's best to assume so."

Amelia nodded and stepped back. "I probably know the factory better than anyone here. Who's the best person to talk to?"

Paul waved to a uniformed officer.

Amelia walked towards the superintendent, who was directing a team to the external staircase at the side of the building.

"You'll want to cover the doors on each level. There's a couple of internal staircases. They're in a poor state of repair, but usable."

"DI Amelia Barton, I presume." He held out his hand, then remembered himself and withdrew it. "DS Brown has filled us in on the internal structure."

Amelia hadn't noticed Catherine. She must have come in one of the other vans. She spotted her next to the road. Amelia waved at her and walked towards her, meeting her halfway. "They called you in?"

"Yeah. I thought the agency would take the lead, but this is Armed Response and the local negotiation team."

"We're just relegated to bystanders." Amelia glanced down and lowered her voice. "I don't suppose you told them about the door on the canal side."

Catherine stared ahead of her and muttered, "No. Did you?"

"You can't see it from this side. And it's so overgrown. Didn't think it was worth bothering them with."

Catherine folded her arms. "We probably should tell them. I mean, we couldn't... what if he's armed?"

"Then he'd have shot the officer at the safe house." Amelia sighed. "Do you think any of these officers will put Cam first?"

"No, but —"

"Someone needs to see that she's protected."

Amelia was surprised that Catherine wasn't arguing with her.

"I can't... my kids…"

Of course, Amelia had kids, too. "Just make sure they don't spot me."

"Okay... just be careful."

Nothing seemed to be happening. Amelia wasn't going to sit by and wait for Cam to be killed. It was The Undertaker's role to stop Cam from talking. Did it matter to him if he killed her before he was taken in? He wasn't getting away, that was for sure.

The partially concealed door could only be reached from the side of the building that backed directly onto the canal. It was surrounded by barbed wire and, as she'd found when fitting the bugging devices months before, only a thin and agile person would be able to reach it. Of course, it could be locked on the inside and the whole thing could be a waste of time. Amelia used her jacket to push aside the barbed edges and gingerly stepped behind the building. The low wall that ran along the side of the factory meant that she was unlikely to be spotted by DI Moreton or the other officers. Their gaze was firmly on the front and opposite side of the building with its fire escape.

Amelia moved one foot at a time along the thin walkway, careful not to slip back onto the barbed wire. Fortunately, some of the mortar had fallen away from the bricks, affording her the occasional handhold. She recognised some of the spots Sean had drilled to install cameras.

It wasn't long before she reached the door. Weeds had grown through some of the bricks, concealing the peeling blue paintwork. Amelia wrenched a few of the weeds in search of a door handle. Above the handle was a Yale lock. She tried the handle but, as expected, the door didn't budge. Amelia had some lock-picking tools that she'd brought from the back of her car in one of her pockets. She'd planned to use this door if the opportunity struck.

It took a degree of patience to get the gears in the old lock to move. A few times she thought she'd got it, just for the barrel to swing back into its original position. But on the fourth time of asking, Amelia heard a satisfying click. She tried the door again but it still didn't swing open. Its path was blocked by debris inside. She pushed against the door with her full weight against her shoulder and was rewarded by movement. Now there was just enough space for Amelia to squeeze her body through.

She'd expected to find herself in the large expanse of the ground floor of the factory but, instead, she was in an abandoned storeroom. The door had been blocked by bolts of fabric that were once brightly patterned but were now a dirty grey. Amelia imagined that the rest of the floor previously housed row upon row of women machinists earning

251

piecemeal wages.

But there was no time to linger. Cam had been spotted on the second floor and Amelia had to get to her as soon as possible.

The staircases were in a state of disrepair with several steps either missing or rotten. Amelia trod carefully, wary of putting weight on each step just in case the wood gave way beneath her, but also not wishing to alert Jason. She didn't really have a plan for what she was going to do when she reached him. Her main aim was to get Cam to safety.

She reached the top of the stairs on the second floor and peered around the corner. There was no sign of Jason, but she spotted Cam. Her hands were tied to a chair and her mouth was stuffed by a scarf. She spotted Amelia, who pressed a finger to her lips. Instead of remaining still, Cam suddenly began to struggle against the ropes, her eyes wild, pleading with Amelia.

Amelia shook her head and raised a finger to her lips once more. Cam took the hint this time and stopped struggling. Amelia needed to find out where Jason was. She improvised sign language for a man and pointed at an eye. Cam didn't move. Amelia tried again but this time pointed in a couple of directions. Cam must have got it this time as she moved her head to the left. It was the one area of the room that Amelia couldn't see without leaving the stairwell. She imagined the bank of windows and Jason standing facing them, watching as the police moved into position. Was he stupid enough to put himself in the line of fire?

Amelia remembered that there were far fewer windows on this floor. The old offices would have been here. They needed light on the downstairs floors so that the seamstresses could see the thread, but it was less important up here.

Amelia turned her back to Cam and pointed, hoping she'd understand that she needed to know which direction Jason was facing. When she turned back to Cam, she nodded. Amelia assumed that this meant that he was looking the other way. There were a few old, battered desks in the room. If she was quick enough, she could use these as cover to get to Cam. Maybe she'd even get the chance to untie her.

It was worth the risk. Without even looking at Jason, she made a dash for the first desk. She slumped down behind it and counted to ten, then raised her head. Jason was standing at the edge of one of the windows, staring out. She could move to the next desk.

Eventually, Amelia reached the last of the desks. Jason turned at the same moment. Had he seen her?

Jason turned back to the window and Amelia breathed out. She waited a moment for her heart to stop racing. Cam stared at her, causing Amelia to shake her head again. The last thing she needed now was for Jason to be alerted to her presence.

Amelia counted to ten again and slowly raised her head above the desk. Jason had moved to the other side of the window, beads of sweat forming on his brow. He must know that this wasn't going to end well, whatever happened.

On her hands and knees, Amelia shuffled towards Cam. As soon as she reached the chair, she began to untie the knot that bound Cam's hands.

A booming voice cut through the silence, causing Amelia to drop to the floor.

"I need you to dial this number." The disembodied voice recited a string of digits.

Jason jumped back from the window and turned back towards the room.

Amelia had already shuffled back behind the desk. Trust DI Moreton to ruin her chance.

The booming voice from the loud hailer repeated the instruction. Amelia waited. Jason showed no sign of doing as he was being asked.

"There's nowhere for you to go. Let's talk."

Jason started to pace the room.

Shit! Amelia thought. This wasn't the best hiding place. She forced herself to raise her head above the desk again.

Jason had his back to her and was wrestling his phone out of his pocket as DI Moreton repeated the number. He dropped the phone and it landed with a clunk.

Cam became more agitated, squirming in the chair. Amelia realised that the rope was now loose. With Jason on edge, the last thing she needed was for Cam to make a run for it.

It was too late. Cam suddenly rose from the chair and, like a sprinter off the blocks headed at full pelt towards the stairs. Jason darted after her. And so did Amelia.

He reached Cam on the first step and lunged for her. She slipped, hurtling down the steps until, with a huge crack, she disappeared from sight. The staircase had given way and Amelia had no idea how far the woman had fallen.

There was no time to think of that now. Jason turned to face her. Either anger or fea spurred him on and he aimed a blow at her. She ducked and charged at him, sending him to the floor inches away from the stairwell.

Though he was winded, he shot up quickly and faced Amelia, breathing heavily.

"You're never going to get away with what you've done," Amelia shouted.

He lurched forward. She side-stepped him and grabbed the chair that Cam had been tied to.

"One death of an officer could be seen as an accident. But two..."

He grabbed the leg of the chair, but she had the upper hand and forced him backwards.

"You could give others up. Maybe get a deal."

Of course, this was stupid. She needed to get closer to the windows so they could see her from below.

Thrusting the chair forward again, she side-stepped. One, two, three steps, then swung the chair in front of her, catching Jason on the arm.

She was nearer to the window now. Just a couple more steps. The booming voice had stopped. Maybe they could see what was happening. So why hadn't anyone entered the building yet?

Jason lunged forward, catching her unawares. She hit the wall behind her hard. Grabbing the chair from her, he held it above his head, but before he could bring it down on her head, she smashed into him, the force of her body pushing him back across the room. He hit a desk and toppled over it. She followed him and raised her hand in a punch. He grabbed her fist. He was much stronger than she expected. The force of the punch was lost and

now she was fighting to retrieve her hand. As
he rolled onto his side, he took her with him
but she managed to get her knee under her and
grabbed a table to drag herself back to her
feet. He shuffled back and stood up.

Behind him were the windows looking out
over the canal. Amelia ran at Jason for a
final time, expecting him to hit the wall
behind — but he didn't. He hit a floor-to-
ceiling window. The force took them both
through it, splintering the glass into a
thousand shards.

Amelia sensed she was falling but could
do nothing to prepare. She hit the water with
an explosive splash and sank straight to the
bottom. The shock and cold forced the breath
out of her lungs.

Amelia remembered Ted's helmsmanship
training. "You'll be fine, Amelia. If you fall
in, just stand up." Slipping on the uneven
floor of the canal, she forced her feet under
her and managed to stand.

She took a deep breath.

Jason hadn't been so lucky. He was
floating face down a few yards away from her.

Looking back up at the building, she
couldn't believe she'd survived the fall. She
grabbed the collar of Jason's T-shirt and
dragged him back to the water's edge. By this
time, several officers were ready to pull him
out of the water.

Amelia pushed up on the edge of the
towpath and Catherine and another officer
grabbed her arms, pulling her clear of the
dirty water. Amelia coughed, spitting out any
water she'd swallowed.

"You could have died, you idiot."
Catherine rubbed her back.

"How's Cam?" Amelia coughed again.

"I'm sure she's fine."

"You've found her? She fell through the stairs." Amelia attempted to stand up, but dizziness overcame her.

"I'm sure we can check once we get you to the hospital."

"I'm not going to any hospital," Amelia insisted.

"Yes, you bloody are." Pat was standing in front of her with a towel in her hands. Before Amelia could even consider where she'd produced it from, Pat bundled it around her and led her to a waiting ambulance.

Chapter 32
Heroes

The last time Amelia had a stay in hospital, the whole family came to visit. This time, not even her work colleagues were allowed in. The kind doctor who checked her over in A&E marvelled at her resilience but also insisted that she stay overnight for tests. He'd reeled off a list of diseases that she might have contracted from ingesting canal water that made even Amelia squirm. He also wanted to check for signs of concussion.

Cam was alive. Amelia knew that much. She'd badgered every nurse and doctor in the place until a harassed nurse finally told her that Cam had a broken pelvis and a head injury, but was expected to recover.

That was all that mattered.

By the evening, Amelia was climbing the walls until she was admonished by a matron. "It's not all about you, you know."

It calmed her for a while as she watched the other patients on the COVID-free ward. They seemed happy enough to be here and thanked the nurses as their temperature and blood pressure was taken. It made her stop and think. The medical staff looked exhausted as they passed from bed to bed.

And here she was complaining. She couldn't imagine what they'd put up with over the last few months.

Then she thought of her mum and the fear she must have felt. Amelia wondered at what point she realised that she might not survive, and who had held her hand as she passed.

A young nurse sat down next to her bed. "I've got some news for you."

Amelia smiled. "Go on," hoping that it was a message from her daughters.

"Jason Bennett, the man you sent flying into the canal is alive and –" the nurse looked up to the ceiling, "– how was it described? Oh yes. He's singing like a canary."

Amelia laughed.

The nurse placed her hand on Amelia's leg. "Bloody. Well. Done! Someone caught your exploits on camera and it's gone viral. You look like some sort of superwoman."

Great. How would she ever live that one down?

Amelia returned to work after a couple of days of being "looked after" at home.

Pat called her straight into her office.

"I thought you'd be working from home."

Her boss looked up and didn't answer. "What I should do is fire you on the spot."

"I'm not sure the police federation would allow that." Amelia smiled. She knew where these conversations went.

"There's some talk of a bravery medal."

"Forget it." Amelia sat down. "I'll just continue as I am and get on with my job. Thanks."

"Jason Bennett's got an infection in his leg. It looks like he might lose it."

Amelia had noticed the gash on his leg when he was dragged from the canal but didn't know how serious it was. Fortunately, she'd tested negative for all water-borne infections, including Weil's disease, which sounded particularly nasty.

Pat continued. "He's saying that someone on the force informed him about the jobs that were available for him to do."

Amelia's ears pricked up. "Did he give a name?"

Pat sighed. "No, just an alias. And a description. It could be anyone."

One of their own. He could even work for the NCA. It could be one of her colleagues.

"Have we looked at Branfield's buddies?" Branfield was still on parole with no court date as yet.

Pat shrugged. "The guy's middle-aged, average height, average build, with greying hair and a slight paunch. How many male officers could that be? Bennet seemed to think he wasn't that high up. But he knows all the top crime bosses. He knows all their secrets."

"Maybe we'll get something more from Cam."

"Maybe. We could do with a break."

Amelia returned to her desk. She'd had a missed call from a non-UK number. She did a search and found that it had originated in Slovakia. Who could it be? She returned the call. It was answered with a cheery "Hello?"

"Hi. This is DI Amelia Barton. Who am I speaking to?"

"Sergeant Curiova. I believe you wanted to speak to me."

Amelia waited for the gears in her brain to catch up. "Yes, sorry – of course. Thanks for ringing."

"So…?"

"I just wanted to say that what you've done is amazing."

The woman didn't speak for a moment. "Sorry?"

"Giving the trafficked women names – for their families."

The line crackled. "It's all I could do these last few months. I'm shielding... cancer."

"You have cancer?"

"Not now. I'm in remission but I can't work in the field as I'm vulnerable. So, I —"

"You fought for them. Each and every one." Each and every one of them who was trafficked, each branded with a rose tattoo and murdered for some bastard's gratification, then displayed like rag dolls by a man who liked to play around with dead bodies.

But this young woman had brought them home.

Amelia held back the tears. "I just wanted to say thank you."

Printed in Great Britain
by Amazon